DOVER
CHILDREN'S THRIFT CLASSICS

North American Indian Tales

W. T. LARNED

Illustrated by John Green

DOVER PUBLICATIONS, INC.
Mineola, New York

DOVER CHILDREN'S THRIFT CLASSICS
GENERAL EDITOR: STANLEY APPELBAUM
EDITOR OF THIS VOLUME: ADAM H. FROST

Copyright

Published in Canada by General Publishing Company, Ltd., 30 Lesmill Road, Don Mills, Toronto, Ontario.

Bibliographical Note

This Dover edition, first published in 1997, is a slightly corrected republication of eight of the nine stories featured in *American Indian Fairy Tales,* first published by P. F. Volland Company, Joliet, Illinois, 1921. The illustrations were prepared specially for this edition.

Library of Congress Cataloging-in-Publication Data

Larned, W. T. (William Trowbridge)
    [American Indian fairy tales]
    North American Indian tales / W.T. Larned ; illustrated by John Green.
       p.   cm. — (Dover children's thrift classics)
    Originally published: American Indian fairy tales. New York : P.F. Volland, [c1921]. With new introd. and ill.
    ISBN 0-486-29656-3 (pbk.)
    1. Indians of North America—Folklore. 2. Fairy tales—North America. I. Green, John, 1948– . II. Title. III. Series.
[E98.F6L3 1997]
398.2'08997—dc21   96-48788
                                                  CIP

Manufactured in the United States of America
Dover Publications, Inc., 31 East 2nd Street, Mineola, N.Y. 11501

Contents

Iagoo won the children's hearts with his stories.

Iagoo, the Story-Teller

THERE NEVER was anyone so wise and knowing as old Iagoo. There never was an Indian who saw and heard so much. He knew the secrets of the woods and fields, and understood the language of birds and beasts. All his life long he had lived out of doors, wandering far in the forest where the wild deer hide, or skimming the waters of the lake in his birch-bark canoe.

Besides the things he had learned for himself, Iagoo knew much more. He knew the fairy tales and the wonder stories told him by his grandfather, who had heard them from *his* grandfather, and so on, away back to the time when the world was young and strange, and there was magic in almost everything.

Iagoo was a great favorite with the children. No one knew better where to find the beautiful, colored shells which he strung into necklaces for the little girls. No one could teach them so well just where to look for the grasses which their nimble fingers wove into baskets. For the boys he made bows and arrows—bows from the ash-tree, that would bend far back without breaking, and arrows, strong and straight, from the sturdy oak.

But most of all, Iagoo won the children's hearts with his stories. Where did the robin get his red breast? How did fire find its way into the wood, so that an Indian can get it out again by rubbing two sticks together? Why was Coyote, the prairie wolf, so much cleverer than the

1

other animals; and why was he always looking behind him when he ran? It was old Iagoo who could tell you where and why.

Now, winter was the time for story-telling. When the snow lay deep on the ground, the North Wind came howling from his home in the Land of Ice, and the cold moon shone from the frosty sky, it was then that the Indians gathered in the wigwam. It was then that Iagoo sat by the fire of blazing logs, and the little boys and girls gathered around him.

"Whoo, whoo!" wailed the North Wind. The sparks leapt up, and Iagoo laid another log on the fire. "Whoo, whoo!" What a mischievous old fellow was this North Wind! One could almost see him—his flowing hair all hung with icicles. If the wigwam were not so strong he would blow it down, and if the fire were not so bright he would put it out. But the wigwam was made on purpose, for just such a time as this; and the forest nearby had logs to last forever. So the North Wind could only gnash his teeth, and say, "Whoo, whoo!"

One little girl, more timid than the rest, would draw nearer and put her hand on the old man's arm. "O, Iagoo," she said, "Just listen! Do you think he can hurt us?"

"Have no fear," answered Iagoo. "The North Wind can do no harm to anyone who is brave and cheerful. He blusters, and makes a lot of noise; but at heart he is really a big coward, and the fire will soon frighten him away. Suppose I tell you a story about it."

And the story Iagoo told we shall now tell to you, the story of how Shin-ge-bis fooled the North Wind.

Shin-ge-bis Fools the North Wind

L ONG, LONG ago, in the time when only a few people lived upon the earth, there dwelt in the North a tribe of fishermen. Now, the best fish were to be found in the summer season, far up in the frozen places where no one could live in the winter at all. For the King of this Land of Ice was a fierce old man called Ka-bib-on-okka by the Indians—meaning in our language, the North Wind.

Though the Land of Ice stretched across the top of the world for thousands and thousands of miles, Ka-bib-on-okka was not satisfied. If he could have had his way there would have been no grass or green trees anywhere; all the world would have been white from one year's end to another, all the rivers frozen tight, and all the country covered with snow and ice.

Luckily there was a limit to his power. Strong and fierce as he was, he was no match at all for Sha-won-dasee, the South Wind, whose home was in the pleasant land of the sunflower. Where Sha-won-dasee dwelt it was always summer. When he breathed upon the land, violets appeared in the woods, the wild rose bloomed on the yellow prairie, and the cooing dove called musically to his mate. It was he who caused the melons to grow, and the purple grapes; it was he whose warm breath ripened the corn in the fields, clothed the forests in green, and made the earth all glad and beautiful. Then, as the summer days grew shorter in the

3

Hour after hour he sat and smoked.

North, Sha-won-dasee would climb to the top of a hill, fill his great pipe, and sit there—dreaming and smoking. Hour after hour he sat and smoked; and the smoke, rising in the form of a vapor, filled the air with a soft haze until the hills and lakes seemed like the hills and lakes of dreamland. Not a breath of wind, not a cloud in the sky; a great peace and stillness over all. Nowhere else in the world was there anything so wonderful. It was Indian Summer.

Now it was that the fishermen who set their nets in the North worked hard and fast, knowing the time was at hand when the South Wind would fall asleep, and fierce old Ka-bib-on-okka would swoop down upon them and drive them away. Sure enough! One morning a thin film of ice covered the water where they set their nets; a heavy frost sparkled in the sun on the bark roof of their huts.

That was sufficient warning. The ice grew thicker, the snow fell in big, feathery flakes. Coyote, the prairie wolf, trotted by in his shaggy white winter coat. Already they could hear a muttering and a moaning in the distance.

"Ka-bib-on-okka is coming!" cried the fishermen. "Ka-bib-on-okka will soon be here. It is time for us to go."

But Shin-ge-bis, the diver, only laughed.

Shin-ge-bis was always laughing. He laughed when he caught a big fish, and he laughed when he caught none at all. Nothing could dampen his spirits.

"The fishing is still good," he said to his comrades. "I can cut a hole in the ice, and fish with a line instead of a net. What do *I* care for old Ka-bib-on-okka?"

They looked at him with amazement. It was true that Shin-ge-bis had certain magic powers, and could change himself into a duck. They had seen him do it; and that is why he came to be called the "diver." But how would this enable him to brave the anger of the terrible North Wind?

"You had better come with us," they said. "Ka-bib-on-okka is much stronger than you. The biggest trees of the forest bend before his wrath. The swiftest river that runs freezes at his touch. Unless you can turn yourself into a bear, or a fish, you will have no chance at all."

But Shin-ge-bis only laughed the louder.

"My fur coat lent me by Brother Beaver and my mittens borrowed from Cousin Muskrat will protect me in the daytime," he said, "and inside my wigwam is a pile of big logs. Let Ka-bib-on-okka come in by my fire if he dares."

So the fishermen took their leave rather sadly; for the laughing Shin-ge-bis was a favorite with them, and, the truth is, they never expected to see him again.

When they were gone, Shin-ge-bis set about his work in his own way. First of all he made sure that he had plenty of dry bark and twigs and pine-needles, to make the fire blaze up when he returned to his wigwam in the evening. The snow by this time was pretty deep, but it froze so hard on top that the sun did not melt it, and he could walk on the surface without sinking in at all. As for fish, he well knew how to catch them through the holes he made in the ice; and at night he would go tramping home, trailing a long string of them behind him, and singing a song he had made up himself:

> "*Ka-bib-on-okka, ancient man,*
> *Come and scare me if you can.*
> *Big and blustery though you be,*
> *You are mortal just like me!*"

It was thus that Ka-bib-on-okka found him, plodding along late one afternoon across the snow.

"Whoo, whoo!" cried the North Wind. "What impudent, two-legged creature is this who dares to linger here long after the wild goose and the heron have winged their way to the south? We shall see who is master in the Land of Ice. This very night I will force my way into his wigwam, put his fire out, and scatter the ashes all around. Whoo, whoo!"

Night came; Shin-ge-bis sat in his wigwam by the blazing fire. And such a fire! Each backlog was so big it would last for a moon. That was the way the Indians, who had no clocks or watches, counted time; instead of weeks or months, they would say "a moon"—the length of time from one new moon to another.

Shin-ge-bis had been cooking a fish, a fine, fresh fish

caught that very day. Broiled over the coals, it was a tender and savory dish; and Shin-ge-bis smacked his lips, and rubbed his hands with pleasure. He had tramped many miles that day; so it was a pleasant thing to sit there by the roaring fire and toast his shins. How foolish, he thought, his comrades had been to leave a place where fish was so plentiful, so early in the winter.

"They think that Ka-bib-on-okka is a kind of magician," he was saying to himself, "and that no one can resist him. It's my own opinion that he's a man, just like myself. It's true that I can't stand the cold as he does; but then, neither can he stand the heat as I do."

This thought amused him so that he began to laugh and sing:

> "Ka-bib-on-okka, frosty man,
>   Try to freeze me if you can.
>   Though you blow until you tire,
>   I am safe beside my fire!"

He was in such a high good humor that he scarcely noticed a sudden uproar that began without. The snow came thick and fast; as it fell it was caught up again like so much powder and blown against the wigwam, where it lay in huge drifts. But instead of making it colder inside, it was really like a thick blanket that kept the air out.

Ka-bib-on-okka soon discovered his mistake, and it made him furious. Down the smoke-vent he shouted; and his voice was so wild and terrible that it might have frightened an ordinary man. But Shin-ge-bis only laughed. It was so quiet in that great, silent country that he rather enjoyed a little noise.

"Ho, ho!" he shouted back. "How are you, Ka-bib-on-okka? If you are not careful you will burst your cheeks."

Then the wigwam shook with the force of the blast,

and the curtain of buffalo hide that formed the doorway flapped and rattled, and rattled and flapped.

"Come on in, Ka-bib-on-okka!" called Shin-ge-bis merrily. "Come on in and warm yourself. It must be bitter
cold outside."

At these jeering words, Ka-bib-on-okka hurled himself against the curtain, breaking one of the buckskin
thongs; and made his way inside. Oh, what an icy
breath!—so icy that it filled the hot wigwam like a fog.

Shin-ge-bis pretended not to notice. Still singing, he
rose to his feet, and threw on another log. It was a fat
log of pine, and it burned so hard and gave out so much
heat that he had to sit a little distance away. From the
corner of his eye he watched Ka-bib-on-okka; and what
he saw made him laugh again. The perspiration was
pouring from his forehead; the snow and icicles in his
flowing hair quickly disappeared. Just as a snowman
made by children melts in the warm sun of March, so
the fierce old North Wind began to thaw! There could
be no doubt of it; Ka-bib-on-okka, the terrible, was melt-
ing! His nose and ears became smaller, his body began
to shrink. If he remained where he was much longer, the
King of the Land of Ice would be nothing better than a
puddle.

"Come on up to the fire," said Shin-ge-bis cruelly.
"You must be chilled to the bone. Come up closer, and
warm your hands and feet."

But the North Wind had fled, even faster than he
came, through the doorway.

Once outside, the cold air revived him, and all his
anger returned. As he had not been able to freeze Shin-
ge-bis, he spent his rage on everything in his path.
Under his tread the snow took on a crust; the brittle
branches of the trees snapped as he blew and snorted;

the prowling fox hurried to his hole; and the wandering coyote sought the first shelter at hand.

Once more he made his way to the wigwam of Shin-ge-bis, and shouted down the flue. "Come out," he called. "Come out, if you dare, and wrestle with me here in the snow. We'll soon see who's master then!"

Shin-ge-bis thought it over. "The fire must have weakened him," he said to himself. "And my own body is warm. I believe I can overpower him. Then he will not annoy me any more, and I can stay here as long as I please."

Out of the wigwam he rushed, and Ka-bib-on-okka came to meet him. Then a great struggle took place.

Then a great struggle took place.

Over and over on the hard snow they rolled, locked in one another's arms.

All night long they wrestled; and the foxes crept out of their holes, sitting at a safe distance in a circle, watching the wrestlers. The effort he put forth kept the blood warm in the body of Shin-ge-bis. He could feel the North Wind growing weaker and weaker; his icy breath was no longer a blast, but only a feeble sigh.

At last, as the sun rose in the east, the wrestlers stood apart, panting. Ka-bib-on-okka was conquered. With a despairing wail, he turned and sped away. Far, far to the North he sped, even to the land of the White Rabbit; and as he went, the laughter of Shin-ge-bis rang out and followed him. Cheerfulness and courage can overcome even the North Wind.

The Little Boy and Girl in the Clouds

IAGOO, THE Story-Teller, was seated one evening in his favorite corner, gazing into the embers of the log fire like one in a dream.

At such a time the children knew better than to interrupt him by asking questions or teasing him for a story. They knew that Iagoo was turning over in his mind the strange things he had heard and the wonderful things he had seen; that the burning logs and red coals took on curious shapes and made odd pictures that only he could understand, and that if they did not disturb him he would presently begin to speak.

On this particular evening, however, though they waited patiently and talked to one another only in low whispers, Iagoo kept on sitting there as if he were made of stone. They began to fear that he had forgotten them, and that bedtime would come without a story. So at last little Morning Glory, who was always asking questions, thought of one she had never asked before.

"Iagoo!" she said; and then she stopped, fearing to offend him.

At the sound of her voice the old man roused himself, as if his mind had been away on a long journey into the past.

"What is it, Morning Glory?"

"Iagoo—can you tell me—were the mountains always here?"

The old man looked at her gravely. No matter how

11

hard the question was, or how unexpected, Iagoo was always glad to answer. He never said: "I'm too busy, don't bother me," or, "Wait till some other time." So when Morning Glory asked him this very peculiar question, he nodded his wise old head, saying:

"Do you know, I've often asked myself that very thing: Were the mountains always here?"

He paused, and looked once more into the fire, as if the answer was to be found there if he only looked long enough. At last he spoke again:

"Yes, I think it must be true that the mountains were always here—the mountains and the hills. They were made when the world was made—a long, long time ago; and the story of how the world was made you have heard before. But there is one high hill that was not always here—a hill that grew like magic, all of a sudden. Did I ever tell you the story of the Big Rock—how it rose and rose, and carried the little boy and girl up among the clouds?"

"No, no!" shouted the children in a chorus. "You never told us that one. Tell it to us now."

And this is the story of the magical Big Rock, as old Iagoo heard it from his grandfather, who heard it from *his* great-grandfather, who was almost old enough to have been there himself when it all happened:

In the days when all animals and men lived on friendly terms, when Coyote, the prairie wolf, was not a bad sort of fellow when you came to know him, and even the Mountain Lion would growl pleasantly and pass you the time of day—there lived in a beautiful valley a little boy and girl.

This valley was a lovely place to live in; never was such a playground anywhere on earth. It was like a great green carpet stretching for miles and miles, and when the wind blew upon the long grass it was like

looking at the waves of the sea. Flowers of all colors
bloomed in the beautiful valley, berries grew thick on
the bushes, and birds filled the summer air with their
songs.

Best of all, there was nothing whatever to fear. The
children could wander at will—watching the gay but-
terflies, making friends with the squirrels and rabbits,
or following the flight of the bee to some tree where his
honey is stored.

As for the wild animals, it was all very different from
what it is to-day, when they keep the poor things in
cages, or coop them up in a little patch of ground behind a high fence. In the beautiful valley the animals ran
free and happily, as they were meant to do. The Bear
was a big, lazy, good-natured fellow, who lived on
berries and wild honey in the summer, and in winter
crept into his cavern in the rocks and slept there till the
spring. The deer were not only gentle, but tame as
sheep, and often came to crop the tender grass that
grew where the two children were accustomed to play.

They loved all the animals, and the animals loved
them; but perhaps their special favorites were Jack
Rabbit and Antelope. Jack Rabbit had long legs, and
long ears—almost as long as a mule's, and no animal of
his size could jump so high. But of course he could not
jump as high as Antelope—the name of a beautiful little
deer, with short horns and slender legs, who could run
like the wind.

Another thing that made the happy valley such a
pleasant place to live in was the river that flowed
through it. All the animals came from miles around to
drink from its clear, cool waters, and to bathe in it on a
hot summer day. One shallow pool seemed made especially for the little boy and girl. Their friend, the Beaver,
with his flat tail like an oar and his feet webbed like a

He clambered up the rock and drew his sister up after him.

duck's, had taught them how to swim almost as soon as
they had learned to walk; and to splash around in the
pool on a warm afternoon was among their greatest
pleasures.

One day in mid-summer the water was so pleasant
that they remained in the pool much longer than usual,
so that when at last they came out they were quite
tired. And as they were a little chilled besides, they
looked around for a good place where they could get
dry and warm.

"Let's climb up on that big, flat rock, with the moss
on it," said the little boy. "We've never done it before. It
would be lots of fun."

So he clambered up the side of the rock, which was
only a few feet high, and drew his sister up after him.

Then they lay down to rest, and pretty soon, without intending it at all, they were fast asleep.

Nobody knows how it happened that exactly at this time the rock began to rise and grow. But it did happen, because there it is today, high and bare and steep, higher than the other hills in the valley. As the children slept, it rose and rose, inch by inch, foot by foot; by the next day it was taller than the tallest trees.

Meanwhile their father and mother were searching for them everywhere, but all in vain; nor was any trace of them to be found. No one had seen them climb up on the rock, and everyone concerned was too much excited to notice what had really happened to it. The parents wandered far and wide saying: "Antelope, have you seen our little boy and girl? Jack Rabbit, *you* must have seen our little boy and girl." But none of the animals had seen them.

At last they met Coyote, the cleverest of them all, trotting along the valley with his nose in the air; so they put the same question to him.

"No," said Coyote. "I have not seen them for a long time. But my nose was given me to smell with, and my brains were given me to think with. So who can tell but that I may help you?"

He trotted by their side, along the banks of the river, and pretty soon they came to the pool where the children had been in swimming. Coyote sniffed and sniffed. He ran around and around, with his nose to the ground; then he ran right up to the rock, put his forepaws up as high as he could reach, and sniffed again.

"H-m-m!" he grunted. "I cannot fly like the Eagle, and I cannot swim like the Beaver. But neither am I stupid like the Bear, nor ignorant like the Jack Rabbit. My nose has never deceived me yet; your little boy and girl must be up there on that rock."

"But how could they get there?" asked the astonished parents. For the rock was now so high that the
top was lost to sight in the clouds.

"That is not the question," said Coyote severely, un-
willing to admit there was anything he did not know.
"That is not the question at all. Anybody could ask that.
The only question worth asking is: How are we to get
them down again?"

So they called all the animals together, to talk it over
and see what could be done. Then the Bear said: "If I
could only put my arms around the rock I could climb
it. But it is much too big for that." And the Fox said: "If
it were only a deep hole, instead of a high hill, I would
be able to help you." And the Beaver said: "If it were
just a place out in the water I could swim to, I'd show
you very quickly."

But as this kind of talk did not take them very far,
they decided to try what jumping would do. There
seemed to be no other way; and as each one was anx-
ious to do his part, the smallest one was permitted to
make the first attempt. So the Mouse made a funny little hop, about as high as your hand. The Squirrel went
a little higher. Jack Rabbit made the highest jump of his
life, and almost broke his back, to no purpose. Antelope
gave a great bound in the air, but managed to light on
his feet again without doing himself any harm. Finally,
the Mountain Lion went a long way off, to get a good
start, ran toward the rock with great leaps, sprang
straight up—and fell and rolled over on his back. He
had made a higher jump than any of them; but it was
not nearly high enough.

No one knew what to do next. It seemed as if the little boy and girl must be left sleeping on forever, up
among the clouds. Suddenly they heard a tiny voice
saying:

"Perhaps if you let *me* try, I might *climb* up the rock."

They all looked around in surprise, wondering who it was that spoke; and at first they could see nobody, and thought that Coyote must be playing a trick on them. But Coyote was as much surprised as anyone.

"Wait a minute. I'm coming as fast as I can," said the tiny voice again. Then a Measuring Worm crawled out of the grass—a funny little worm that made its way along by hunching up its back and drawing itself ahead an inch at a time.

"Ho, ho!" said the Mountain Lion, from deep down in his throat. He always spoke that way when his dignity was offended. "Ho, ho! Did you ever hear of such impudence? If I, a lion, have failed, how can a miserable little crawling worm like you hope to succeed; just tell me that!"

"Perhaps if you let me *try, I might* climb *up the rock."*

"It's downright silly," said Jack Rabbit. "That's what it is. I never heard of such conceit."

However, after much talk, they agreed at last that it could do no harm to let him try. So the Measuring Worm made his way slowly to the rock, and began to climb. In a few minutes he was higher than Jack Rabbit had jumped. Soon he was farther up than the lion had been able to leap: before long he had climbed out of sight.

It took the Measuring Worm a whole month, climbing day and night, to reach the top of the magic rock. When he got there he awakened the little boy and girl, who were much surprised to see where they were, and guided them safely down along a path no one else knew anything about. Thus, by patience and perseverance, the weak little creature was able to do something that the Bear, for all his size, and the Lion, for all his strength, could never have done at all. That was a long time ago; today there are no more lions or bears in the valley, and no one ever thinks of them. But everybody thinks of the Measuring Worm, because the Big Rock is still there, and the Indians have named it after him. Tu-tok-a-nu-la, they call it, a big name indeed for a little fellow, yet by no means too big when you come to think of the big, brave thing he did.

The Child of the Evening Star

ONCE UPON a time, on the shores of the great lake, Gitchee Gumee, there lived a hunter who had ten beautiful young daughters. Their hair was dark and glossy as the wings of the blackbird, and when they walked or ran it was with the grace and freedom of the deer in the forest.

Thus it was that many suitors came to court them—brave and handsome young men, straight as arrows, fleet of foot, who could travel from sun to sun without fatigue. They were sons of the prairie, wonderful horsemen who would ride at breakneck speed without saddle or stirrup. They could catch a wild horse with a noose, tame him in a magical way by breathing into his nostrils, then mount him and gallop off as if he always had been ridden. There were those also who came from afar in canoes, across the waters of the Great Lake, canoes which shot swiftly along, urged by the strong, silent sweep of the paddle.

All of them brought presents with which they hoped to gain the father's favor. Feathers from the wings of the eagle who soars high up near the sun; furs of fox and beaver and the thick, curly hair of the bison; beads of many colors, and wampum, the shells which the Indians used for money; the quills of the porcupine and the claws of the grizzly bear; deerskin dressed to such a softness that it crumpled up in the hands—these and many other things they brought.

One by one, the daughters were wooed and married, until nine of them had chosen husbands. One by one, other tents were ·reared, so that instead of the single family lodge on the shores of the lake there were tents enough to form a little village. For the country was a rich one, and there was game and fish enough for all.

There remained the youngest daughter, Oweenee— the fairest of them all. Gentle as she was beautiful, none was so kind of heart. Unlike her proud and talkative elder sisters, Oweenee was shy and modest, and spoke but little. She loved to wander alone in the woods, with no company but the birds and squirrels and her own thoughts. What these thoughts were we can only guess; from her dreamy eyes and sweet expression, one could but suppose that nothing selfish or mean or hateful ever came into her mind. Yet Oweenee, modest though she was, had a spirit of her own. More than one suitor had found this out. More than one conceited young man, confident that he could win her, went away crestfallen when Oweenee began to laugh at him.

The truth is, Oweenee seemed hard to please. Suitor after suitor came—handsome, tall young men, the handsomest and the bravest in all the country round. Yet this fawn-eyed maiden would have none of them. One was too tall, another too short; one too thin, another too fat. At least, that was the excuse she gave for sending them away. Her proud sisters had little patience with her. It seemed to be questioning their own taste; for Oweenee, had she said the word, might have gained a husband more attractive than any of theirs. Yet no one was good enough. They could not understand her; so they ended by despising her as a silly and unreasonable girl.

Her father, too, who loved her dearly and wished her to be happy, was much puzzled. "Tell me, my daughter,"

There came into the village an Indian named Osseo.

he said to her one day, "Is it your wish never to marry? The handsomest young men in the land have sought you in marriage, and you have sent them all away— often with a poor excuse. Why is it?"

Oweenee looked at him with her large, dark eyes.

"Father," she said at last. "It is not that I am wilful. But it seems somehow as if I had the power to look into the hearts of men. It is the heart of a man, and not his face, that really matters; and I have not yet found one youth who in this sense is really beautiful."

Soon after, a strange thing happened. There came into the little village an Indian named Osseo, many years older than Oweenee. He was poor and ugly, too. Yet Oweenee married him.

How the tongues of her nine proud sisters did wag! Had the spoiled little thing lost her mind? they asked. Oh, well! They always knew she would come to a bad end; but it was pretty hard on the family.

Of course they could not know what Oweenee had seen at once—that Osseo had a generous nature and a heart of gold; that beneath his outward ugliness was the beauty of a noble mind, and the fire and passion of a poet. That is why Oweenee loved him; knowing, too, that he needed her care, she loved him all the more.

Now, though Oweenee did not suspect it, Osseo was really a beautiful youth on whom an evil spell had been cast. He was in truth the son of the King of the Evening Star—that Evening Star which shines so gloriously in the western sky, just above the rim of the earth, as the sun is setting. Often on a clear evening it hung suspended in the purple twilight like some glittering jewel. So close it seemed, and so friendly, that the little children would reach out their hands, thinking that they might grasp it ere it was swallowed by the night, and keep it always for their own. But the older ones would say: "Surely it must be a bead on the garments of the Great Spirit as he walks in the evening through the garden of the heavens."

Little did they know that the poor, despised Osseo had really descended from that star. And when he, too, stretched out his arms toward it, and murmured words they could not understand, they all made sport of him.

There came a time when a great feast was prepared in a neighboring village, and all of Oweenee's kinsfolk were invited to attend. They set out on foot—the nine proud sisters, with their husbands, walking ahead, much pleased with themselves and their finery, and all chattering like magpies. But Oweenee walked behind in silence, and with her walked Osseo.

The sun had set; in the purple twilight, over the edge of the earth, sparkled the Evening Star. Osseo, pausing, stretched out his hands toward it, as if imploring pity; but when the others saw him in this attitude they all made merry, laughing and joking and making unkind remarks.

"Instead of looking up in the sky," said one of the sisters, "he had better be looking on the ground. Else he may stumble and break his neck." Then calling back to him, she cried: "Look out! Here's a big log. Do you think you can manage to climb over it?"

Osseo made no answer; but when he came to the log he paused again. It was the trunk of a huge oak-tree blown down by the wind. There it had lain for years, just as it fell; and the leaves of many summers lay thick upon it. There was one thing, though, the sisters had not noticed. The tree-trunk was not a solid one, but hollow, and so big around that a man could walk inside it from one end to the other without stooping.

But Osseo did not pause because he was unable to climb over it. There was something mysterious and magical in the appearance of the great hollow trunk; and he gazed at it a long time, as if he had seen it in a dream, and had been looking for it ever since.

"What is it, Osseo?" asked Oweenee, touching him on the arm. "Do you see something that I cannot see?"

But Osseo only gave a shout that echoed through the forest, and leaped inside the log. Then as Oweenee, a little alarmed, stood there waiting, the figure of a man came out from the other end. Could this be Osseo? Yes, it was he—but how transformed! No longer bent and ugly, no longer weak and ailing; but a beautiful youth— vigorous and straight and tall. His enchantment was at an end.

But the evil spell had not been wholly lifted, after all.

A great change was taking place in his loved one.

As Osseo approached he saw that a great change was taking place in his loved one. Her glossy black hair was turning white, deep wrinkles lined her face; she walked with a feeble step, leaning on a staff. Though he had regained his youth and beauty, she in turn had suddenly grown old.

"O, my dearest one!" he cried. "The Evening Star has mocked me in letting this misfortune come upon you. Better far had I remained as I was; gladly would I have borne the insults and laughter of your people rather than you should be made to suffer."

"As long as you love me," answered Oweenee, "I am perfectly content. If I had the choice to make, and only one of us could be young and fair, it is you that I would wish to be beautiful."

Then he took her in his arms and caressed her, vowing that he loved her more than ever for her goodness of heart; and together they walked hand in hand, as lovers do.

When the proud sisters saw what had happened they could scarcely believe their eyes. They looked enviously at Osseo, who was now far handsomer than any one of their husbands, and much their superior in every other way. In his eyes was the wonderful light of the Evening Star, and when he spoke all men turned to listen and admire him. But the hard-hearted sisters had no pity for Oweenee. Indeed, it rather pleased them to see that she could no longer dim their beauty, and to realize that people would no longer be singing her praises in their jealous ears.

The feast was spread, and all made merry but Osseo. He sat like one in a dream, neither eating nor drinking. From time to time he would press Oweenee's hand, and speak a word of comfort in her ear. But for the most part he sat there, gazing through the door of the tent at the star-besprinkled sky.

Soon a silence fell on all the company. From out of the night, from the dark, mysterious forest, came the sound of music—a low, sweet music that was like, yet unlike, the song sung by the thrush in summer twilight. It was magical music such as none had ever heard, coming, as it seemed, from a great distance, and rising and falling on the quiet summer evening. All those at the feast wondered as they listened. And well they might! For what to them was only music, was to Osseo a voice that he understood, a voice from the sky itself, the voice of the Evening Star. These were the words that he heard:

"Suffer no more, my son; for the evil spell is broken, and hereafter no magician shall work you harm. Suffer no more; for the time has come when you shall leave the earth and dwell here with me in the heavens. Before you is a dish on which my light has fallen, blessing it and giving it a magic virtue. Eat of this dish, Osseo, and all will be well."

So Osseo tasted the food before him, and behold! The tent began to tremble, and rose slowly into the air; up, up above the tree-tops—up, up toward the stars. As it rose, the things within it were wondrously changed. The kettles of clay became bowls of silver, the wooden dishes were scarlet shells, while the bark of the roof and the poles supporting it were transformed into some glittering substance that sparkled in the rays of the stars. Higher and higher it rose. Then the nine proud sisters and their husbands were all changed into birds. The men became robins, thrushes and wood-peckers. The sisters were changed into various birds with bright plumage; the four who had chattered most, whose tongues were always wagging, now appeared in the feathers of the magpie and bluejay.

Osseo sat gazing at Oweenee. Would she, too, change into a bird, and be lost to him? The very thought of it made him bow his head with grief; then, as he looked at her once more, he saw her beauty suddenly restored, while the color of her garments was the color only to be found where the dyes of the rainbow are made.

Again the tent swayed and trembled as the currents of the air bore it higher and higher, into and above the clouds; up, up, up—till at last it settled gently on the land of the Evening Star.

Osseo and Oweenee caught all the birds, and put them in a great silver cage, where they seemed quite content in each other's company. Scarcely was this

The King of the Evening Star came to greet them.

done when Osseo's father, the King of the Evening Star, came to greet them. He was attired in a flowing robe, spun from star-dust, and his long white hair hung like a cloud upon his shoulders.

"Welcome," he said, "my dear children. Welcome to the kingdom in the sky that has always awaited you. The trials you have passed through have been bitter; but you have borne them bravely, and now you will be rewarded for all your courage and devotion. Here you will live happily; yet of one thing you must beware."

He pointed to a little star in the distance—a little, winking star, hidden from time to time by a cloud of vapor.

"On that star," he continued, "lives a magician named Wabeno. He has the power to dart his rays, like so many arrows, at those he wishes to injure. He has always been my enemy; it was he who changed Osseo into an old man and cast him down upon the earth. Have a care that his light does not fall upon you. Luckily, his power for evil has been greatly weakened; for the friendly clouds have come to my assistance, and form a screen of vapor through which his arrows cannot penetrate."

The happy pair fell upon their knees, and kissed his hands in gratitude.

"But these birds," said Osseo, rising and pointing to the cage. "Is this also the work of Wabeno, the magician?"

"No," answered the King of the Evening Star. "It was my own power, the power of love, that caused your tent to rise and bear you hither. It was likewise by my power that the envious sisters and their husbands were transformed into birds. Because they hated you and mocked you, and were cruel and scornful to the weak and the old, I have done this thing. It is not so great a punishment as they deserve. Here in the silver cage they will be happy enough, proud of their handsome plumage, strutting and twittering to their hearts' content. Hang the cage there, at the doorway of my dwelling. They shall be well cared for."

Thus it was that Osseo and Oweenee came to live in the kingdom of the Evening Star; and, as the years passed by, the little winking star where Wabeno, the magician, lived grew pale and paler and dim and dimmer, till it quite lost its power to harm. Meanwhile a little son had come to make their happiness more perfect, a charming boy with the dark, dreamy eyes of his mother and the strength and courage of Osseo.

It was a wonderful place for a little boy to live in—close to the stars and the moon, with the sky so near that it seemed a kind of curtain for his bed, and all the glory of the heavens spread out before him. But sometimes he was lonely, and wondered what the Earth was like—the Earth his father and mother had come from. He could see it far, far below—so far that it looked no bigger than an orange; and sometimes he would stretch out his hands toward it, just as the little children on earth stretch out their hands for the moon.

His father had made him a bow, with little arrows, and this was a great delight to him. But still he was lonely, and wondered what the little boys and girls on earth were doing, and whether they would be nice to play with. The Earth must be a pretty place, he thought, with so many people living on it. His mother had told him strange stories of that far-away land, with its lovely lakes and rivers, its great, green forests where the deer and the squirrel lived, and the yellow, rolling prairies swarming with buffalo.

These birds, too, in the great silver cage had come from the Earth, he was told; and there were thousands and thousands just like them, as well as others even more beautiful that he had never seen at all. Swans with long, curved necks, that floated gracefully on the waters; whip-poor-wills that called at night from the woods; the robin redbreast, the dove and the swallow. What wonderful birds they must be!

Sometimes he would sit near the cage, trying to understand the language of the feathered creatures inside. One day a strange idea came into his head. He would open the door of the cage and let them out. Then

"Come back, I tell you!" he cried.

they would fly back to Earth, and perhaps they would take him with them. When his father and mother missed him they would be sure to follow him to the Earth, and then—

He could not quite see just how it would all end. But he found himself quite close to the cage, and the first thing he knew he had opened the door and let out all the birds. Round and round they flew; and now he was half sorry, and a little afraid as well. If the birds flew back to Earth, and left him there, what would his grandfather say?

"Come back, come back!" he called.

But the birds only flew around him in circles, and paid no attention to him. At any moment they might be winging their way to the Earth.

"Come back, I tell you!" he cried, stamping his foot and waving his little bow. "Come back, I say, or I'll shoot you."

Then, as they would not obey him, he fitted an arrow to his bow and let it fly. So well did he aim that the arrow sped through the plumage of a bird, and the feathers fell all around. The bird itself, a little stunned but not much hurt, fell down; and a tiny trickle of blood stained the ground where it lay. But it was no longer a bird, with an arrow in its wing; instead, there stood in its place a beautiful young woman.

Now, no one who lives in the stars is ever permitted to shed blood, whether it be of man, beast or bird. So when the few drops fell upon the Evening Star, everything was changed. The boy suddenly found himself sinking slowly downward, held up by invisible hands, yet ever sinking closer and closer to the Earth. Soon he could see its green hills and the swans floating on the water, till at last he rested on a grassy island in a great lake. Lying there, and looking up at the sky, he could see the tent descending, too. Down it softly drifted, till it in turn sank upon the island; and in it were his father and mother, Osseo and Oweenee—returned to earth, to live once more among men and women and teach them how to live. For they had learned many things in their life upon the Evening Star; and the children of Earth would be better for the knowledge.

As they stood there, hand in hand, all the enchanted birds came fluttering after, falling and fluttering through the air. Then as each one touched the Earth, it was no longer a bird they saw, but a human being. A human being, yet not quite as before; for now they were only dwarfs, Little People, or Pygmies; Puk-Wudjies, as the Indians called them. Happy Little People they became, seen only by a few. Fishermen, they say, would sometimes get a glimpse of them—dancing in the light of the Evening Star, of a summer night, on the sandy, level beach of the Great Lake.

The Boy Who Snared the Sun

A DEEP, CRUSTED snow covered the earth, and sparkled in the light of a wintry moon. The wind had died away; it was very cold and still. Not a sound came from the forest; the only noise that broke the perfect quiet of the night was the cracking of the ice on the Big-sea-water, Gitchee Gumee, which was now frozen solid.

But inside old Iagoo's teepee it was warm and cheerful. The teepee, as the Indians call a tent, was covered with the thick, tough skin of the buffalo; the winter coat of Muk-wa, the bear, had now become a pleasant soft rug for Iagoo's two young visitors, Morning Glory and her little brother, Eagle Feather. Squatting at their ease on the warm fur, they waited for the old man to speak.

Suddenly a white-footed mouse crept from his nest in a corner, and, advancing close to the children, sat up on his hind-legs, like a dog that begs for a biscuit. Eagle Feather raised his hand in a threatening way, but Morning Glory caught him by the arm.

"No, no!" she said. "You must not harm him. See how friendly he is, and not a bit afraid. There is game enough in the forest for a brave boy's bow and arrow. Why should he spend his strength on a weak little mouse?"

Eagle Feather, pleased with anything that seemed like praise of his strength, let his hand fall.

"Your words are true words, Morning Glory," he answered. "Against Ahmeek, the beaver, or Wau-be-se, the wild swan, it is better that I should measure my hunter's skill."

At this, Iagoo, turning around, broke his long silence. "There was a time," he said, mysteriously, "when a thousand boys such as Eagle Feather would have been no match at all for that mouse as he used to be."

"When was that?" asked Eagle Feather, looking uneasily at his sister.

"In the days of the great Dormouse," answered Iagoo. "In the days, long ago, when there were many more animals than men on the earth, and the biggest of all the beasts was the Dormouse. Then something strange happened—something that never happened before or since. Shall I tell you about it?"

"O, please do!" begged Morning Glory.

"The story I am going to tell you," began Iagoo, "is not so much a story about the Dormouse as it is a story about a little boy and his sister. Yet had it not been for the Dormouse, I would not be here to tell about it, and you would not be here to listen.

- "To begin with, you must understand that the world in those days was a different sort of place from what it is now. O yes, a different sort of place. People did not eat the flesh of animals. They lived on berries, and roots, and wild vegetables. The Great Spirit, who made all things on land, and in the sky and water, had not yet given men Mon-da-min, the Indian corn. There was no fire to give them heat, or to cook with. In all the world there was just one small fire, watched by two old witches who let nobody come near it; and until Coyote, the prairie wolf, came along and stole some of this fire, the food that people could manage to get was eaten raw, the way it grew."

"They must have been pretty hungry," said Morning Glory.

"O, yes, they were hungry," agreed Iagoo. "But that was not all. There were so many animals, and so few men, that the animals ruled the earth in their own way. The biggest of them all was Bosh-kwa-dosh, the Mastodon. He was higher than the highest trees, and he had an enormous appetite. But he did not stay long on earth, or there would not have been food enough even for the other animals."

"I thought you said the Dormouse was the biggest," interrupted Eagle Feather.

Iagoo looked at him severely.

"At the time I speak of," he continued, "Bosh-kwa-dosh, the Mastodon, had just gone away. He had not gone a bit too soon, either; for, by this time, the only people left on the whole earth were a young girl and her little brother."

"Like Eagle Feather and me?" asked Morning Glory.

"The girl was much like you," said Iagoo, patiently. "But the boy was a dwarf, who never grew to be more than three feet high. Being so much stronger and larger than her brother, she gathered all the food for both, and cared for him in every way. Sometimes she would take him along with her, when she went to look for berries and roots. 'He's such a very little boy,' she said to herself, 'that if I leave him all alone, some big bird may swoop down, and carry him off to its nest.'

"She did not know what a strange boy he was, and how much mischief he could do when he set his mind upon it. One day she said to him: 'Look, little brother! I have made you a bow and some arrows. It is time you learned to take care of yourself; so when I am gone, practice shooting, for this is a thing you must know how to do.'

"Winter was coming, and to keep himself from freezing the boy had nothing better than a light garment

woven by his sister from the wild grasses. How could
he get a warm coat? As he asked himself that question,
a flock of snow birds flew down, near by, and began
pecking at the fallen logs, to get the worms. 'Ha!' said
he. 'Their feathers would make me a fine coat.' Bending
his bow, he let an arrow fly; but he had not yet learned
how to shoot straight. It went wide of the mark. He shot
a second, and a third; then the birds took fright, and
flew away.

"Each day he tried again—shooting at a tree when
there was nothing better to aim at. At last he killed a
snow bird, then another and another. When he had
shot ten birds, he had enough. 'See, sister,' he said, 'I

The boy never grew to be more than three feet high.

shall not freeze. Now you can make me a coat from the skins of these little birds.'

"So his sister sewed the skins together, and made him the coat, the first warm winter coat he had ever had. It was fine to look at, and the feathers kept out the cold. Eh-yah! he was proud of it! With his bow and arrows, he strutted up and down, like a little turkey cock. 'Is it true?' he asked, 'that you and I are the only persons living on earth? Perhaps if I look around, I may find someone else. It will do no harm to try.'

"His sister feared he would come to some harm; but he had made up his mind to see the world for himself, and off he went. But his legs were short, he was not used to walking far, and he soon grew tired. When he came to a bare place, on the edge of a hill, where the sun had melted the snow, he lay down, and was soon fast asleep.

"As he slept, the sun played him a trick. It was a mild winter's day. The bird skins of which the coat was made were still fresh and tender, and under the full glare of the sun they began to shrivel and shrink. 'Eh-yah! What's wrong?' he muttered in his sleep, feeling the coat become tighter and tighter. Then he woke, stretched out his arms, and saw what had happened.

"The sun was nearly sinking now. The boy stood up and faced it, and shook his small fist. 'See what you have done!' he cried, with a stamp of his foot. 'You have spoiled my new birdskin coat. Never mind! You think yourself beyond my reach, up there; but I'll be revenged on you. Just wait and see!'"

"But how could he reach the sun?" asked Morning Glory, her eyes growing rounder and rounder.

"That is what his sister asked, when he told her about it," said Iagoo. "And what do you think he did? First, he did nothing at all but stretch himself out on the ground, where he lay for ten days without eating or moving. Then he turned over on the other side, and lay there for ten days more. At last he rose to his feet. 'I have made up my mind,' he said. 'Sister, I have a plan to catch the sun in a noose. Find me some kind of a cord from which I can make a snare.'

"She got some tough grass, and twisted it into a rope. 'That will not do,' he said. 'You must find something stronger.' He no longer talked like a little boy, but like one who was to be obeyed. Then his sister thought of her hair. She cut enough from her head to make a cord, and when she had plaited it he was much pleased, and said it would do. He took it from her, and drew it between his lips, and as he did this it turned into a kind of

The boy stood up and shook his small fist.

metal, and grew much stronger and longer, till he had so much that he wound it around his body.

"In the middle of the night he made his way to the hill, and there he fixed a noose at the place where the sun would rise. He had to wait a long time in the cold and darkness. But at last a faint light came into the sky. As the sun rose it was caught fast in the noose, and there it stayed."

Iagoo stopped talking, and sat looking into the fire. One might have supposed that when he did this he saw pictures in the flames, and in the red coals, and that these pictures helped him to tell the story. But Morning Glory was impatient to hear the rest.

"Iagoo," she said, timidly, at last. "Did you forget about the Dormouse?"

"Eh-yah! the Dormouse! No. I have not forgotten," answered the old man, rousing himself. "When the sun did not rise as usual, the animals could not tell what had happened. Ad-ji-dau-mo, the squirrel, chattered and scolded from the branch of a pine tree. Kah-gah-gee, the raven, flapped his wings, and croaked more hoarsely than ever, to tell the others that the end of the world had come. Only Muk-wa, the bear, did not mind. He had crept into his cave for the winter, and the darker it was the better he liked it.

"Wa-bun, the East Wind, was the one who brought the news. He had drawn from his quiver the silver arrows with which he chased the darkness from the valleys. But the sun had not risen to help him, and the arrows fell harmless to the earth. 'Wake, wake!' he wailed. 'Someone has caught the sun in a snare. Which of all the animals will dare to cut the cord?'

"But even Coyote, the prairie wolf, who was the wisest of them all, could think of no way to free the sun. So great was the heat thrown out by its rays that he could not come within an arrow's flight of where it was caught fast in the magical noose of hair.

"'Leave it to me!' screamed Ken-eu, the war-eagle, from his nest on the cliff. 'It is I alone who soar to the sky, and look the sun in the face, without winking. Leave it to me!'

"Down he darted through the darkness, and up he flew again, with his eagle feathers singed. Then they woke the Dormouse. They had a hard time doing it, because when he once went to sleep he stayed asleep for six months, and it was almost impossible to arouse him. Coyote crept close to his ear, and howled with all his might. It would have split the eardrum of almost any other animal. But Kug-e-been-gwa-kwa, the Dormouse, only groaned and turned over on the other side, and Coyote had a narrow escape from being mashed flat, like a corn-cake.

"'There is only one thing that will wake him,' said Coyote, getting up and shaking himself. 'I will run to the mountain cave of An-ne-mee-kee, the Thunder. His voice is even more terrible than mine.' So off he went at a gallop.

"Soon they could hear An-ne-mee-kee coming. Boom, boom! When he shouted in the ear of the Dormouse, the biggest beast on earth rose slowly to his feet. In the darkness he looked bigger than ever, almost as big as a mountain. An-ne-mee-kee, the Thunder, shouted once more, to make sure that the Dormouse was really wide awake, and would not go to sleep again.

"'Now,' said Coyote to the Dormouse, 'it is you that will have to free the sun. If he burned one of us, there would be little left but bones. But you are so big that if part of you is burned away there will still be enough. Then, in that case you would not have to eat so much, or work so hard to get it.'

"The Dormouse was a stupid animal, and Coyote's talk seemed true talk. Besides, as he was the biggest animal, he was expected to do the biggest things. So he made his way to the hill, where the little boy had snared the sun, and began to nibble at the noose. As he nibbled away, his back got hotter and hotter. Soon it began to burn, till all the upper part of him burned away, and became great heaps of ashes. At last, when

All that was left was an animal no larger than an ordinary mouse.

he had cut through the cord with his teeth, and set the sun free, all that was left of him was an animal no larger than an ordinary mouse. What he became then, so he is today. Still, he is big enough for a mouse; and perhaps that is what Coyote really meant. Coyote, the prairie wolf, is a cunning beast, up to many tricks, and it is not always easy to tell exactly what he means."

How the Summer Came

MORNING GLORY was tired of the winter, and longed for the spring to come. Sometimes it seemed as if Ka-bib-on-okka, the fierce old North Wind, would never go back to his home in the Land of Ice. With his cold breath he had frozen tight and hard the Big-Sea-Water, Gitchee Gumee, and covered it deep with snow, till you could not tell the Great Lake from the land.

Except for the beautiful green pines, all the world was white—a dazzling, silent world in which there was no musical murmur of waters and no song of birds.

"Will O-pee-chee, the robin, never come again?" sighed Morning Glory. "Suppose there was no summer anywhere, and no Sha-won-dasee, the South Wind, to bring the violet and the dove. O, Iagoo, would it not be dreadful?"

"Be patient, Morning Glory," answered the old man. "Soon you will hear Wa-wa, the wild goose, flying high up, on his way to the North. I have lived many moons. Sometimes he seems long in coming, but he always comes. When you hear him call, then O-pee-chee, the robin, will not be far behind."

"I'll try to be patient," said Morning Glory. "But Ka-bib-on-okka, the North Wind, is so strong and fierce. I can't help wondering whether there ever was a time when his power was so great that he made his home here always. It makes me shiver to think of it!"

Iagoo rose from his place by the fire, and drew to one side the curtain of buffalo-hide that screened the doorway. He pointed to the sky—clear, and sparkling with stars.

"Look!" he said. "There, in the North. See that little cluster of stars. Do you know the name we give it?"

"*I* know," said Eagle Feather. "It is O-jeeg An-nung—the Fisher stars. If you look right, you can see how they make the body of the Fisher. He is stretched out flat, with an arrow through his tail. See, sister!"

"The Fisher," repeated Morning Glory. "You mean the furry little animal, something like a fox? Is Marten another name for it?"

"That's it," said Eagle Feather.

"Yes, I see," nodded Morning Glory. "But why is the Fisher spread out flat that way, in the sky, with an arrow sticking through his tail?"

"I don't know just exactly why," admitted Eagle Feather. "I suppose some hunter was chasing him. Perhaps Iagoo can tell us."

Iagoo closed the curtain, and went back to the fire.

"You thought there might have been a time when there was no summer on the earth," he said to Morning Glory. "And you were right. Until O-jeeg, the Fisher, found a way to bring the summer down from the sky, the earth was everywhere covered with snow, and it was always cold. If O-jeeg had not been willing to give his life, so that all the rest of us could be warm, Ka-bib-on-okka, the North Wind, would have ruled the world, as he now rules the Land of Ice."

Then Morning Glory and Eagle Feather sat down on the soft rug that was once the winter coat of Muk-wa, the bear, and Iagoo told them the story of How the Summer Came:

In the wild forest that borders the Great Lake there

There once lived a mighty hunter named O-jeeg.

once lived a mighty hunter named O-jeeg. No one knew the woods so well as he; where others would be lost without a trail to guide them, he found his way easily and quickly, by day or night, through the trackless tangle of trees and underbrush. Where the red deer fled, he followed; the bear could not escape his swift pursuit. He had the cunning of the fox, the endurance of the wolf, the speed of the wild turkey when it runs at the scent of danger.

When O-jeeg shot an arrow, it always hit the mark. When he set out on a journey, no storm or snow could turn him back. He did everything he said he would do, and did it well.

Thus it was that some men came to believe that O-jeeg was a Manito—the Indian name for one who has magic powers. This much was certain: whenever O-jeeg wished to do so, he could change himself into the little animal known as the Fisher, or Marten.

Perhaps that is why he was on such friendly terms with some of the animals, who were always willing to help him when he called upon them. Among these were the otter, the beaver, the lynx, the badger and the wolverine. There came a time, as we shall see, when he needed their services badly, and they were not slow in coming to his assistance.

O-jeeg had a wife whom he dearly loved, and a son, of thirteen years, who promised to be as great a hunter as his father. Already he had shown great skill with the bow and arrow; if some accident should prevent O-jeeg from supplying the family with the game upon which they lived, his son felt sure that he himself could shoot as many squirrels and turkeys as they needed to keep them from starving. With O-jeeg to bring them venison, bear's meat and wild turkey, they had thus far plenty to eat. Had it not been for the cold, the boy would have been happy enough. They had warm clothing, made from deerskin and furs; to keep their fire burning, they had all the wood in the forest. Yet, in spite of this, the cold was a great trial; for it was always winter, and the deep snow never melted.

Some wise old men had somewhere heard that the sky was not only the roof of our own world, but also was the floor of a beautiful world beyond; a land where birds with bright feathers sang sweetly through a pleasant, warm season called Summer. It was a pretty story that people wished to believe; and likely enough, they said, when you came to think that the sun was so far away from the earth, and so close to the sky itself.

The boy used to dream about it, and wonder what could be done. His father could do anything; some men said he was a Manito. Perhaps he could find some way to bring Summer to the earth. That would be the greatest thing of all.

Sometimes it was so cold that when the boy went into the woods his fingers would be frost-bitten. Then he could not fit the notch of his arrow to the bowstring, and was obliged to go back home without any game whatever. One day he had wandered far in the forest, and was returning empty-handed, when he saw a red squirrel seated on his hind legs on the stump of a tree. The squirrel was gnawing a pine cone, and did not try to run away when the young hunter came near. Then the little animal spoke:

"My grandson," said he, "there is something I wish to tell you that you will be pleased to hear. Put away your arrows, and do not try to shoot me, and I shall give you some good advice."

The boy was surprised; but he unstrung his bow, and put the arrow in his quiver.

"Now," said the squirrel, "listen carefully to what I have to say. The earth is always covered with snow, and the frost bites your fingers, and makes you unhappy. I dislike the cold as much as you do. To tell the truth, there is little enough for me to eat in these woods, with the ground frozen hard all the time. You can see how thin I am, for there is not much fat in a pine cone. If someone could manage to bring the Summer down from the sky, it would be a great blessing."

"Is it really true, then," asked the boy, "that up beyond the sky is a pleasant warm land, where Winter only stays for a few moons?"

"Yes, it is true," said the squirrel. "We animals have known it for a long time. Ken-eu, the war-eagle, who soars near the sun, once saw a small crack in the sky. The crack was made by Way-wass-i-mo, the Lightning, in a great storm that covered all the earth with water. Ken-eu, the war-eagle, felt the warm air leaking through; but the people who live up above mended the crack the very next moment, and the sky has never leaked again."

"Then our wise old men were right," said the boy. "O-jeeg, my father, can do most anything he has a mind to. Do you suppose if he tried hard enough, he could get through the sky, and bring the Summer down to us?"

"Of course!" exclaimed the squirrel. "That is why I spoke to you about it. Your father is a Manito. If you beg him hard enough, and tell him how unhappy you are, he is sure to make the attempt. When you go back, show him your frost-bitten fingers. Tell him how you tramp all day through the snow, and how difficult it is to make your way home. Tell him that some day you may be frozen stiff, and never get back at all. Then he will do as you ask, because he loves you very much."

The boy thanked the squirrel, and promised to follow this advice. From that day he gave his father no peace. At last O-jeeg said to him:

"My son, what you ask me to do is a dangerous thing, and I do not know what may come of it. But my power as a Manito was given me for a good purpose, and I can put it to no better use than to try to bring the Summer down from the sky, and make the world a more pleasant place to live in."

Then he prepared a feast to which he invited his friends, the otter, the beaver, the lynx, the badger, and the wolverine; and they all put their heads together, to decide what was best to be done. The lynx was the first to speak. He had travelled far on his long legs, and had

They all put their heads together, to decide what was to be done.

been to many strange places. Besides, if you had good strong eyes, and you looked at the sky, on a clear night when there was no moon, you could see a little group of stars which the wise old men said was exactly like a lynx. It gave him a certain importance, especially in matters of this kind; so when he began to speak, the others listened with great respect.

"There is a high mountain," said he, "that none of you has ever seen. No one ever saw the top, because it is always hidden by the clouds; but I am told it is the highest mountain in the world, and almost touches the sky."

The otter began to laugh. He is the only animal that can do this; sometimes he laughs for no particular reason, unless it is that he thinks himself more clever than the other animals, and likes to "show off."

"What are you laughing at?" asked the lynx.

"Oh, nothing," answered the otter. "I was just laughing."

"It will get you into trouble some day," said the lynx. "Just because you never heard of this mountain, you think it is not there."

"Do you know how to get to it?" asked O-jeeg. "If we could climb to the top, we might find a way to break through the sky. It seems a good plan."

"That is what I was thinking," said the lynx. "It is true I don't know just where it is. But a moon's journey from here, there lives a Manito who has the shape of a giant. *He* knows, and he could tell us."

So O-jeeg bade good-bye to his wife and his little son, and the next day the lynx began the long journey, with O-jeeg and the others following close behind. It was just as the lynx had said. When they had travelled, day and night, for a moon, they came to a lodge, as the white men call an Indian's tent; and there was the Manito standing in the doorway. He was a queer-looking man, such as they had never seen before, with an enormous head and three eyes, one eye being set in his forehead above the other two.

He invited them into the lodge, and set some meat before them; but he had such an odd look, and his movements were so awkward, that the otter could not help laughing. At this, the eye in the Manito's forehead grew red, like a live coal, and he made a leap at the otter, who barely managed to slip through the doorway, out into the bitter cold and darkness of the night, without having tasted a morsel of supper.

When the otter had gone, the Manito seemed satisfied, and told them they could spend the night in his lodge. They did so; and O-jeeg, who stayed awake while his friends slept, noticed that only two of the Manito's

Only two of the Manito's eyes were closed.

eyes were closed, while the one in his forehead remained wide open.

In the morning the Manito told O-jeeg to travel
straight toward the North Star, and that in twenty
suns—the Indian name for days—they would reach the
mountain. "As you are a Manito yourself," he said, "you
may be able to climb to the top, and to take your
friends with you. But I cannot promise that you will be
able to get down again."

"If it is close enough to the sky," answered O-jeeg,
"that is all I ask."

Once more they set out. On their way they met the
otter, who laughed again when he saw them; but this

time he laughed because he was glad to find them, and glad to get some meat that O-jeeg had saved from the Manito's supper.

In twenty days they came to the foot of the mountain. Then up and up they climbed, till they passed quite through the clouds; up once more, till at last they stopped, all out of breath, and sat down to rest on the highest peak in the world. To their great delight, the sky seemed so close that they could almost touch it.

O-jeeg and his comrades filled their pipes. But before smoking, they called out to the Great Spirit, asking for success in their attempt. In Indian fashion they pointed to the earth, to the sky overhead, and to the four winds.

"Now," said O-jeeg, when they had finished smoking, "which of you can jump the highest?"

The otter grinned.

"Jump, then!" commanded O-jeeg.

The otter jumped, and, sure enough, his head hit the sky. But the sky was the harder of the two, and back he fell. When he struck the ground, he began to slide down the mountain; soon he was out of sight, and they saw him no more.

"Ugh!" grunted the lynx. "He is laughing on the other side of his mouth."

It was the beaver's turn. He, too, hit the sky, but fell down in a heap. The badger and the lynx had no better luck, and their heads ached for a long time afterward.

"It all depends on you," said O-jeeg to the wolverine. "You are the strongest of them all. Ready, now—jump!"

The wolverine jumped, and fell, but came down on his feet, sound and whole.

"Good!" cried O-jeeg. "Try again!"

This time the wolverine made a dent in the sky.

"It's cracking!" exclaimed O-jeeg. "Now, once more!"

For the third time the wolverine jumped. Through

the sky he went, passing out of sight, and O-jeeg quickly followed him.

Looking around them, they beheld a beautiful land. O-jeeg, who had spent his life among the snows, stood like a man who dreams, wondering if it could be true. He had left behind him a bare world, white with winter, whose waters were always frozen, a world without song or color. He had now come into a country that was a great green plain, with flowers of many hues; where birds of bright plumage sang amid the leafy branches of trees hung with golden fruit. Streams wandered through the meadows, and flowed into lovely lakes. The air was mild, and filled with the perfume from a million blossoms. It was Summer.

Along the banks of a lake were the lodges in which lived the people of the sky, who could be seen some

O-jeeg stood, wondering if it could be true.

distance away. The lodges were empty, but before them were hung cages in which there were many beautiful birds. Already the warm air of Summer had begun to rush through the hole made by the wolverine, and O-jeeg now made haste to open the cages, so that the birds could follow.

The sky-dwellers saw what was happening, and raised a great shout. But Spring, Summer and Autumn had already escaped through the opening into the world below, and many of the birds as well.

The wolverine, too, had managed to reach the hole, and descend to the earth, before the sky-dwellers could catch him. But O-jeeg was not so fortunate. There were still some birds remaining that he knew his son would like to see, so he went on opening the cages. By this time the sky-dwellers had closed the hole, and O-jeeg was too late.

As the sky-dwellers pursued him, he changed himself into the Fisher, and ran along the plain, toward the North, at the top of his speed. In the form of the Fisher he could run faster. Also, when he took this shape, no arrow could injure him unless it hit a spot near the tip of his tail.

But the sky-dwellers ran even faster, and the Fisher climbed a tall tree. They were good marksmen, and they shot a great many arrows, until at last one of these chanced to hit the fatal spot. Then the Fisher knew that his time had come.

Now he saw that some of his enemies were marked with the totems, or family arms, of his own tribe. "My Cousins!" he called to them. "I beg of you that you go away, and leave me here alone."

The sky-dwellers granted his request. When they had gone, the Fisher came down from the tree, and wandered around for a time, seeking some opening in the plain through which he might return to the earth. But there was no opening; so at last, feeling weak and faint, he stretched himself flat on the floor of the sky, through which the stars may be seen from the world below.

"I have kept my promise," he said with a sigh of content. "My son will now enjoy the summer, and so will all the people who dwell on the earth. Through the ages to come I shall be set as a sign in the heavens, and my name will be spoken with praise. I am satisfied."

So it came about that Fisher remained in the sky, where you can see him plainly for yourself, on a clear night, with the arrow through his tail. The Indians call them the Fisher Stars—O-jeeg An-nung; but to white men they are known as the constellation of the Plough.

Grasshopper

THERE WAS once a merry young Indian who could jump so high, and who played so many pranks, that he came to be known as Grasshopper. He was a tall, handsome fellow, always up to mischief of one kind or another; and though his tricks were sometimes amusing, he carried them much too far, and so in time he came to grief.

Grasshopper owned all the things that an Indian likes most to have. In his lodge were all sorts of pipes and weapons, ermine and other choice furs, deer-skin shirts wrought with porcupine quills, many pairs of beaded moccasins, and more wampum belts than one person could have honestly come by.

The truth is, Grasshopper did not get these things by his skill and courage as a hunter. He got them by shaking pieces of colored bone and wood in a wooden bowl, then throwing them on the ground. That is to say, Grasshopper was a gambler, and such a lucky gambler that he easily won from others, with his game of Bowl and Counters, the things that they had obtained by risking their lives in the hunt.

If people put up with his ways, and even laughed at some of his mad pranks, it was because he could dance so well. Never had there been such a dancer. Was there a wedding to be celebrated, or some feast following a successful hunt—then who but Grasshopper could so well supply the entertainment?

54

Then Grasshopper became a kind of human whirlwind.

He could dance with a step so light that it seemed to leave no mark upon the earth. He could dance as the Indian dances when he goes to war, or as when he holds a festival in honor of the corn. But the dance in which he excelled was a furious, dizzy dance, with leaps and bounds, that fairly turned the heads of the beholders.

It was then that Grasshopper became a kind of human whirlwind. As he spun round and round, his revolving body drew up the dry leaves and the dust, till the dancer all but faded from view, and you saw instead what looked like a whirling cloud.

Once, when the great Manito, named Man-a-bo-zho, took a wife and came to live with the tribe, that he might teach them best how to live, Grasshopper danced at the wedding. The Beggar's Dance, he called it, and such a dance! On the shores of the Big-Sea-Water, Gitchee Gumee, are heaps of sand rising into little hills known as dunes. Had you asked Iagoo, he would have told you that these dunes were the work of Grasshopper, who whirled the sands together, and piled them into hills, as he spun madly around in his dance at Man-a-bo-zho's wedding.

But though Grasshopper came to the wedding, and danced this crazy Beggar's Dance, it seems probable that he did it more to please himself, and to show his skill, than to honor the great Man-a-bo-zho. Grasshopper really had no respect for anybody. When Iagoo's grandfather was in the middle of some interesting story, and had come to the most exciting part, Grasshopper likely as not would yawn and stretch himself, and say in a loud whisper that he had heard it all before.

So, too, with Man-a-bo-zho. This great Manito, who was the son of the West Wind, Mud-je-kee-wis, had magic powers which he used for the good of the tribe. It was he who fasted and prayed, that his people might be given food other than the wild things of the woods; and whose prayer was answered with the gift of the Indian corn. Then when Kah-gah-gee, King of Ravens, flew down with his band of black thieves, to tear up the seed in the ground, it was Man-a-bo-zho who snared him, and tied him fast to the ridge-pole of his lodge, to croak out a warning to the others.

But Man-a-bo-zho's goodness and wisdom had little effect on Grasshopper. "Pooh!" he would say. "Why should an Indian bother his head with planting corn, when he can draw his bow and kill a good fat deer?" Then he shook his wolf-skin pouch, and rattled the pieces of bone and wood. "As long as I have these," he said to himself, "I need nothing more. After all, it is everybody else that works for the man who knows how to use his head."

He walked through the village, very proud and straight, with his fan of turkey-feathers, a swan's plume fastened in his long, black hair, and the tails of foxes trailing from his heels. In his white deer-skin shirt, edged with ermine, his leggings and moccasins ornamented with beads and porcupine quills, he cut a fine figure. There was to be a dance that night, and Grasshopper, who was a great dandy and a favorite with all the young girls and women, had decked himself out for the occasion. He had painted his face with streaks of blue and vermilion; his blue-black hair, parted in the middle, and glistening with oil, hung to his shoulders in braids plaited with sweet grass. The warriors might call him Shau-go-daya, a coward, and make jokes at his expense, but he did not care. Could he not beat them all when it came to playing ball or quoits, and were not the maidens all in love with his good looks?

Meanwhile, Grasshopper wished to pass the time in some pleasant way. Glancing through the door of a lodge, he saw a group of young men seated on the ground, listening to one of old Iagoo's stories.

"Ha!" he cried. "Have you nothing better to do? Here's a game worth playing."

He drew from his pouch the thirteen pieces of bone and wood, and juggled them from one hand to the other. But no one paid any attention to him. After all,

Grasshopper had "more brains in his heels than in his head." For once he had been too cunning; fearing his skill, no one could be found who would play with him.

"Pooh!" muttered Grasshopper, as he turned away. "I see how it is. The pious Man-a-bo-zho has been preaching to them again. This village is getting to be pretty tiresome to live in. It's about time for me to strike out, and find a place where the young men don't sit around and talk to the squaws."

He walked along, bent on mischief. Even the dance was forgotten; he wondered what he could do to amuse himself. As he came to the outskirts of the village, he passed the lodge of Man-a-bo-zho. "I would like to play him some trick," he said, under his breath, "so he will remember me when I am gone." But he was well aware that Man-a-bo-zho was much more powerful than himself; so he hesitated, not knowing exactly what to do.

At last he walked softly to the doorway, and listened, but could near no sound of voices. "Good!" he said with a grin. "Perhaps nobody is at home." With that, he spun around the outside of the lodge, on one leg, raising a great cloud of dust. No one came out; but on the ridge-pole of the lodge, the captive Kah-gah-gee, King of Ravens, flapped his big black wings, and screamed with a hoarse, rasping cry.

"Fool!" cried Grasshopper. "Noisy fool!"

With a bound, he leapt clear over the lodge, and then back again; at which the raven screamed more harshly than ever. But within the lodge all was silent.

Grasshopper grew bolder. Going to the doorway again, he rattled the flap of buffalo hide. Nobody answered; so, cautiously drawing the curtain to one side, he ventured to peer in. Then he chuckled softly. The lodge was empty.

"This is my chance!" he exclaimed. "Man-a-bo-zho is

Kah-gah-gee flapped his big black wings and screamed.

away, and so is his foolish wife. I'll just pay my respects before they come back, and then I'll be off for good."

Saying this, he went in, and began to turn everything upside down. He threw all the bowls and kettles in a corner, filled the drinking gourds with ashes from the fire, flung the rich furs and embroidered garments this way and that, and strewed the floor with wampum belts and arrows. When he finished, one might have thought a crazy man had been there. No woman in the village was more neat and orderly than the wife of Man-a-bo-zho, and Grasshopper knew this would vex her more than anything else he could do.

"Now for Man-a-bo-zho," he grinned as he left the lodge, well pleased with the mischief he had wrought.

"Caw, caw!" screamed the King of Ravens.

"Kaw!" answered Grasshopper, mocking him. "A pretty sort of pet *you* are. Does Man-a-bo-zho keep you sitting there because you are so handsome? Or is it your beautiful voice?"

With that, he made a leap to the ridge-pole, seized the raven by the neck, and whirled it round and round till it was quite limp and lifeless. Then he left it hanging there, as an insult to Man-a-bo-zho.

He was now in high good humor, and went his way through the forest, whistling and singing, and turning hand-springs to amuse the squirrels. There was a high rock, overlooking the lake, from the top of which one could view the country for miles and miles. Grasshopper climbed it. He could see the village plainly, so he thought he would wait there till Man-a-bo-zho came home. That would be part of the joke.

As he sat there, many birds darted around him, flying close over his head. Man-a-bo-zho called these fowls of the air his chickens, and he had put them under his protection. But Grasshopper had grown reckless. Along came a flock of mountain chickens, and he strung his bow, and shot them as they flew, for no better reason than because they were Man-a-bo-zho's, and not because he needed them for food. Bird after bird fell, pierced by his arrows; when they had fallen, he would throw their bodies down the cliff, upon the beach below.

At last Kay-oshk, the sea-gull, spied him at this cruel sport, and gave the alarm. "Grasshopper is killing us," he called. "Fly, brothers! Fly away, and tell our protector that Grasshopper is slaying us with his arrows."

When Man-a-bo-zho heard the news, his eyes flashed fire, and he spoke in a voice of thunder:

"Grasshopper must die for this! He cannot escape

me. Though he fly to the ends of the earth, I shall follow, and visit my vengeance upon him."

On his feet he bound his magic moccasins with which, at each stride, he could step a full mile. On his hands he drew his magic mittens with which, at one blow, he could shatter the hardest rock. Then he started in pursuit.

Grasshopper had heard the warning call of the seagull, and knew it was time to be off. He, too, could run. So fleet of foot was he that he could shoot an arrow ahead of him, and reach the spot where it fell before it dropped to earth. Also, he had the power to change himself into other shapes, and it was almost impossible to kill him. If, for example, he entered the body of a beaver, and the beaver was slain, no sooner had its flesh grown cold than the *Jee-bi*, or spirit, of Grasshopper would leave the dead body, and Grasshopper would become a man again, ready for some new adventure.

But at first he trusted to his legs and to his cunning. On rushed Man-a-bo-zho, breathing vengeance; swiftly, like a moving shadow, fled Grasshopper. Through the forest and across the hills he fled, faster than the hare. His pursuer was hot on the trail. Once he came upon the forest bed where the grass was still warm and bent; but the Grasshopper, who had rested there, was far away. Once Man-a-bo-zho, high on a mountain, spied him in the meadow below. Grasshopper had shown himself on purpose, and mocked the great Manito, and defied him. The truth is, Grasshopper was just a bit conceited.

At last he grew tired of running. Not that his legs ached him or his feet were sore. But this kind of life was not much to his liking, and he kept his eye open for something new. Pretty soon he came to a stream where the water was backed up by some kind of a dam, so that it flooded the banks. Grasshopper had run about a thousand miles that day—counting all the turns and twists. He was hot and dusty, and the pond, with its water-lilies and rushes, looked cool and refreshing. From far, far away came a faint sound; it was the voice of Man-a-bo-zho, shouting his war-cry.

"Tiresome fellow!" said Grasshopper. "I could almost wish I were a beaver, and lived down there at the bottom of the pond, where no one would disturb me."

Then up popped the head of a beaver, who looked at him suspiciously.

"Don't be alarmed. I left my bow and arrows over there in the grass," explained Grasshopper. "Besides, I was just thinking I would like to be a beaver myself. What do you say to that?"

"I shall have to consult Ahmeek, our chief," answered the friendly animal.

Down he dived to the bottom, and pretty soon Ahmeek's head appeared above the water, followed by the heads of twenty others.

"Let me be one of you," said Grasshopper. "You have a pleasant home down there in the clear, cool water, and I am tired of the life I lead."

Ahmeek was pleased that such a strong, handsome young Indian should wish to join their company.

"But I can help you," he answered, "only after you have plunged into the pond. Do you think you can change yourself into one of us?"

"That is easy," said Grasshopper.

He waded into the water up to his waist; and behold! he had a broad flat tail. Deeper and deeper he went; as the water closed above his head he became a beaver, with glossy, black fur, and feet webbed like a duck's. Down he sank with the others to the bottom, which was covered with heaps of logs and branches.

As the water closed over his head he became a beaver.

"That," explained Ahmeek, "is the food we have stored for the winter. We eat the bark, and you will soon be as fat as any of us."

"But I want to be even fatter," said Grasshopper. "Fatter and ten times as big."

"As you please," agreed Ahmeek. "We can help to make you just as big as you wish."

They reached the lodge where the beavers lived, and entered the doorway, leading into a number of large rooms. Grasshopper selected the largest one for himself.

"Now," he said, "bring me all the food I can eat, and when I am big enough I will be your chief."

The beavers were willing. They set to work getting quantities of the juiciest bark for Grasshopper, who was delighted with this lazy life, and did little more than eat or sleep. Bigger and bigger he grew, till at last he was ten times the size of Ahmeek, and could barely manage to move around in his lodge. He was perfectly happy.

But one day the beaver who kept watch up above, among the rushes of the pond, came swimming to the lodge in a state of great excitement.

"The hunters are after us," he panted. "It is indeed Man-a-bo-zho himself, with his hunters. They are breaking down our dam!"

Even as he spoke, the water in the pond sank lower and lower; the next moment came the tramping of feet, as the hunters leapt upon the roof of the lodge, trying to break it open.

All the beavers but Grasshopper scampered out of the lodge, and escaped into the stream, where they hid themselves in some deep pools, or swam far down with the current. Grasshopper did his best to follow them, but could not. The doorway was too small for his big, fat body; when he attempted to go through it, he found himself stuck fast.

Then the roof gave way, and the head of an Indian appeared.

"*Ty-au!*" he called. "*Tut-ty-au!* See what's here! This must be Me-shau-mik, the King of the Beavers."

Man-a-bo-zho came, and gave one look.

"It's Grasshopper!" he cried. "I can see through his tricks. It's Grasshopper in the skin of a beaver."

Then they fell upon him with their clubs; and eight tall Indians, having swung his limp carcass upon poles, carried it off in triumph through the woods.

But his *Jee-bi*, or spirit, was still in the body of the

beaver, and struggled to escape. The Indians bore him to their lodges and prepared to make a feast. Then, when the squaws were ready to skin him, his flesh was quite cold, and the spirit of Grasshopper left the beaver's body, and glided swiftly away. As the shadowy shape fled across the prairie, into the forest, the watchful Man-a-bo-zho saw it take the human form of Grasshopper, and he started in pursuit.

Grasshopper's life among the beavers had made him lazier than ever, and as he ran he looked around for some easier way than running. Soon he came upon a herd of elk, a species of deer with large, spreading

The doorway was too small for his big, fat body.

horns. The elk were feeding contentedly, and looked sleek and fat.

"They lead a free and happy life," said Grasshopper as he watched them. "Why fatigue myself with running? I'll change myself into an elk, and join their band."

Horns sprouted from his head; in a few minutes the transformation was complete. Still he was not satisfied.

"I am hardly big enough," he said to the leader. "My feet are much too small, and my horns should be twice the size of yours. Is there nothing I can do to make them grow?"

"Yes," answered the leader of the elks. "But you do it at your own risk."

He took Grasshopper into the woods, and showed him a bright red berry that hung in clusters on some small, low bushes.

"Eat these," he said, "and nothing else, and your horns and feet will soon be much bigger than ours. However, it would be wise if you did not eat too many of them."

The berries were delicious. Grasshopper felt that he could not get enough, and he ate them greedily whenever he could find them. Before long his feet had grown so large and heavy he could hardly keep up with the herd, while his horns had such a huge spread that he sometimes found them rather in his way.

One cold day the herd went into the woods for shelter; pretty soon some of the elks who had lingered behind came rushing by with snorts of alarm. Hunters were pursuing them.

"Run!" called out the leader to Grasshopper. "Follow us out on the prairie, where the Indians cannot catch us."

Grasshopper tried to follow them; but his big feet weighted him down, and he ran slowly. Then, as he

Hunters were pursuing them.

plunged madly through a thicket, his spreading horns were entangled in some low branches that held him fast. Already several arrows had whizzed by him; another pierced his heart, and he sank to the ground.

Along came the hunters, with a whoop. "Ty-au!" they exclaimed when they saw the enormous elk. "It is he who made the large tracks on the prairie. Ty-au!"

As they were skinning him, Man-a-bo-zho joined the party; and at that moment the *Jee-bi,* or spirit, of Grasshopper escaped through the mouth of the dead elk, and passed swiftly to the open plains, like a puff of white smoke driven before the wind. Then, as Man-a-bo-zho watched it melt away, he saw once more the mortal shape of Grasshopper; and once more he followed after, breathing vengeance.

As Grasshopper ran on, a new thought came into his head. Above him in the clear blue sky the birds wheeled and soared. "There is the place for me," he said, "far up in the sky. Let me have wings, and I can laugh at Man-a-bo-zho."

Ahead of him was a lake; approaching it, he saw a flock of wild geese known as brant, feeding among the rushes. "Ha," said Grasshopper, admiring them as they sailed smoothly here and there. "They will soon be winging their way to the North. I would like to fly in their company."

He spoke to them, calling them Pish-ne-kuh, his brothers, and they consented to receive him as one of the flock. So he floated on his back till feathers sprouted on him, and he became a brant, with a broad black beak, and a tail that would guide him through the air as a rudder steers a ship.

Greedy as ever, he fed long after the others had had enough, so that he soon grew into the biggest brant ever seen. His beak looked like the paddles of a canoe; when he spread his wings they were as large as two large *au-puk-wa,* or mats. The wild geese gazed at him in astonishment. "You must fly in the lead," they said.

"No," answered Grasshopper. "I would rather fly behind."

"As you please," they told him. "But you will have to be careful. By all means keep your head and neck straight out before you, and do not look down as you fly, or you may meet with an accident."

It was a beautiful sight to see them flap their wings, stretch their long necks, and rise with a "whir" from the lake, mounting the wind, and rushing on before it. They flew with a breeze from the south, faster and faster, till their speed was like the flight of an arrow.

One day, passing over a village, they could hear the people shouting. The Indians were amazed at the size of the big brant, flying in the rear of the flock; yelling as loud as they could yell, their cries made Grasshopper curious. One voice especially seemed familiar to him, and he could not resist the temptation to draw in his neck and stretch it down toward the earth. As he did so, the strong wind caught his tail, and turned him over and over. In vain he tried to recover his balance; the wind whirled him round and round, as it whirls a leaf. The earth came nearer, the shouts of the Indians grew louder in his ears; at last he fell with a thud, and lay lifeless.

It was a fine feast of wild goose that had dropped so suddenly from the skies. The hungry Indians pounced upon him, and began to pluck his feathers. This was the very village where Grasshopper had once lived; little had he dreamed that he would ever return to supply it with such a dinner, a dinner at which he himself was to be the best dish.

But again his *Jee-bi,* or spirit, went forth, and fled in the form of Grasshopper; again Man-a-bo-zho, shouting his war-cry, followed after.

Grasshopper had now come to the desert places, where there were few trees, and no signs of animal life. Man-a-bo-zho was gaining on him; he must play some new trick. Coming at last to a tall pine-tree growing in the rock, he climbed it, pulled off all the green needles, and scattered them about, leaving the branches quite bare. Then he took to his heels again. When Man-a-bo-zho came, the pine spoke to him, saying:

"See what Grasshopper has done. Without my foliage

I am sure to die. Great Manito, I pray you give me back my green dress."

Man-a-bo-zho, who loves and protects all trees, had pity on the pine. He collected the scattered needles, and restored them to the branches. Then he hastened on with such speed that he overtook Grasshopper, and put his hand out to clutch him. But Grasshopper stepped quickly aside, and spun round and round on one leg in his whirlwind dance, till the air all about was filled with leaves and sand. In the midst of this whirl-wind he sprang into a hollow tree, and changed himself into a snake. Then he crept out through the roots, and not a moment too soon; for Man-a-bo-zho smote the tree with one of this magic mittens, and crumbled it to powder.

Grasshopper changed himself back into his human form, and ran for dear life. The only thing left for him to do was to hide. But where? In his headlong flight he had come again to the shores of the Great Lake; and he saw rising before him the high cliff of the Picture Rocks. If he could but manage to reach these rocks, the Manito of the Mountain, who lived in one of the gloomy cav-erns, might let him in. Sure enough! As he reached the cliff, calling out for help, the Manito opened the door, and told him to enter.

Hardly had the big door closed with a bang, than along came Man-a-bo-zho. With his mitten he gave a tap on the rock that made the splinters fly.

"Open!" he cried, in a terrible voice.

But the Manito was brave and hospitable.

"I have sheltered you," he said to Grasshopper, "and I would rather die myself than give you up."

Man-a-bo-zho waited, but no answer came.

"As you will," he said at last. "If the door is not

He gave a tap on the rock that made the splinters fly.

opened to me by night, I shall call upon the Thunder
and the Lightning to do my bidding."

The hours passed; darkness fell. Then from a black
cloud that had gathered over the Great Lake, Way-wass-
i-mo, the red-eyed Lightning, shot his bolts of fire.
Crash—boom—crash! An-ne-mee-kee, the Thunder,
shouted hoarsely from the heavens. A wild wind arose;
the trees of the forest swayed and groaned, and the
foxes hid in their holes.

Way-wass-i-mo, the Lightning, leapt from the black
cloud, and darted at the cliff. The rock trembled; the
door was shivered, and fell apart. Out from his gloomy

cavern came the Manito of the Mountain, asking Man-a-
bo-zho for mercy. It was granted, and the Manito fled to
the hills.

Grasshopper then appeared; the next moment he
was buried under a mass of rock shaken loose by An-
ne-mee-kee, the Thunder. This time he had been killed
in his human form, he could play his mad pranks no
more.

But Man-a-bo-zho, the merciful, remembered that
Grasshopper was not wholly bad.

"Your *Jee-bi,"* he said, "must no longer remain upon
the earth in any form whatever. As a man you lived an
idle, foolish life, and you are no longer wanted here. Instead, I shall permit you to inhabit the skies."

Saying this, he took the ghost of Grasshopper, and
clothed it with the shape of the war-eagle, bidding him
to be chief of all the fowls.

But Grasshopper, the mischievous, is not forgotten
by the people. In the late winter days, snow fine as powder fills the air like a vapor. It keeps the hunter from his
traps, the fisherman from his hole in the ice. Suddenly
a puff of wind seizes this light, powdery snow, blows it
round and round, and sets it whirling along; and when
this happens, the Indians laugh and say:

"Look! There goes Grasshopper. See how well he
dances."

Mish-o-sha, the Magician

IN THE heart of the great green forest once lived a hunter whose lodge was many miles distant from the wigwams of his tribe. His wife had long since died, and he dwelt there all alone with his two young sons, who grew up as best they could without a mother's care.

When the father was away on a hunting trip, the boys had no companions but the birds and beasts of the forest, and with some of the smaller animals they became fast friends. Ad-ji-dau-mo, the squirrel, scampering from tree to tree, would let his nut-shells fall plump on the roof of the lodge. That was his way of knocking at the door, coming to pay a morning call. He was a great talker, without much to say—as is often so with those whose voices are seldom still. But he was bright and merry, chattering away cheerfully about nothing in particular; and it made no difference whether you listened to him or not.

Wa-bo-se, the little white hare, was another friend. One winter's day, when forest food was scarce, O-ne-o-ta, the lynx, was just about to pounce upon him, when the boys' father let fly an arrow—and O-ne-o-ta was no longer interested in little white hares.

Wa-bo-se was grateful for this, and sometimes in his shy way he tried to show it.

The father and the boys lived mostly on big game, like bear and venison. This meat would be cut in strips, and cured; sometimes it had to last them many a long day, when game was scarce, or the woods so dry for want of rain that the twigs would snap under the hunter's feet, and warn the animals he was coming. So the boys were used to being left alone for weeks at a time, when their father was absent.

Then came a season of famine. No berries grew on the bushes, grass withered on the stalk, few acorns hung on the oaks. Some of the brooks went dry. Thus it happened that the hunter had gone far in search of game.

Many months passed. When Seegwun, the elder boy, saw that but little meat remained, he said to his younger brother Ioscoda:

"Let us take what meat is left, and strike out through the forest, toward the North. I remember our father saying that many moons distant lies a great lake called Gitchee Gumee, whose waters are alive with fish."

"But can we find our way?" asked Ioscoda, doubtfully.

"Never fear!" called out a voice from overhead.

It was Ad-ji-dau-mo, the squirrel, frisky as ever, though a little lean for lack of nuts.

"I'll go along with you," he continued, "and so will Wa-bo-se, the white hare. He can hop ahead and find the trail, and I can jump from tree to tree, and keep a look-out. Between us, we are bound to go right."

It proved to be a good idea, and Wa-bo-se took the lead. Where the trail was overgrown with grass, he would nose his way along the ground, without once going wrong; where the track was plain, he would run ahead, then stop and sit up on his haunches, to wait for the boys, his long ears pricked up and moving, to detect the slightest danger.

But nothing happened to alarm them. The lynx, the wildcat and the wolf had all fled before the famine, and the silent forest was empty of savage beasts. On and on they went, till it seemed as if the woods would never end. Then, one day, Ad-ji-dau-mo climbed a tall pine, from whose topmost bough he could see far over the forest. The sun was shining bright; as he cocked his eye and looked toward the north, something that seemed to meet the sky sparkled like silver. It was Gitchee Gumee, the Great Lake.

They had reached a place where nuts were plentiful, and many green things grew that would fatten the white hare. So Wa-bo-se and the squirrel bade good-bye to the boys, who could now make their way with ease. Soon they came to the edge of the woods. They heard a piping cry. It was Twee-tweesh-ke-way, the plover, flying along the beach; in another moment the great glittering waters lay before them.

Seegwun with his sharp hunting knife cut a limb from an ash-tree, and made a bow; from an oak bough he whittled some arrows, which he tipped with flint. He found feathers fallen from a gull's wing for the shaft; a strip cut from his deer-skin shirt supplied the bowstring. Then giving the bow and arrow to Ioscoda, to practice with, he gathered some seed pods from the wild rose, to stay their hunger.

An arrow, badly aimed by his brother, fell into the lake, and Seegwun waded in, to recover it. He had walked into the water till it reached his waist, and put out his hand to grasp the arrow, when suddenly, as if by magic, a canoe came skimming along like a bird. In the canoe was an ugly old man, who reached out, seized the astonished boy, and pulled him on board.

"If I must go with you, take my brother, too!" begged Seegwun. "If he is left here, all alone, he will starve."

But Mish-o-sha, the Magician, only laughed. Then striking the side of the canoe with his hand, and uttering the magic words, *Chemaun Poll*, it shot across the

"My daughters," said the old man to Seegwun.

lake like a thing alive, so that the beach was quickly lost to sight. Soon it came to rest on a sandy shore, and Mish-o-sha, leaping out, beckoned him to follow.

They had landed on an island. Before them, in a grove of cedars, were two wigwams, or lodges; from the smaller one two lovely young girls came out, and stood looking at them.

To Seegwun, who had never before seen a girl, these maidens looked like spirits from the skies. He gazed at them in wonder, half expecting they would vanish. For their part they looked at him without smiling; in their dark eyes were only sympathy and sadness.

"My daughters!" said the old man to Seegwun, with a chuckle that displayed his long, yellow teeth. Then turning to the girls:

"Are you not glad to see me safely back?" he asked,

"and are you not pleased with my handsome young friend here?"

They bent their heads politely, but said nothing.

"It's a long time since you were favored with such a visitor," he went on, in a loud whisper to the elder girl. "He would make you a fine husband."

The maiden murmured something under her breath, and Mish-o-sha gave her a wicked look.

"We shall see, we shall see!" he muttered to himself, laughing like a magpie, and rubbing his long, bony hands together.

Seegwun, much troubled in mind, and hardly knowing what to make of it all, resolved to keep his eyes open. Luckily Mish-o-sha was sometimes careless. He walked on ahead, and entered his lodge, leaving the others together; whereupon the elder girl, approaching Seegwun, spoke to him quickly:

"We are not his daughters," she said. "He brought us here as he brought you. He hates the human race. Every moon he seizes a young man, and pretends he has borne him here as a husband for me. But soon he takes him off in his canoe, and the young man never comes back. We feel sure Mish-o-sha has made away with them all."

"What must I do?" asked Seegwun. "I care less for myself than for my little brother. He was left behind on a wild beach, and may die of hunger."

"Ah!" said the maiden. "You are really good and unselfish; so, no matter what comes of it, we must aid you. Ko-ko-ko-ho, the great owl, keeps watch all night on the bare limb of that big cedar. Wait till Mish-o-sha falls asleep, then wrap yourself from head to foot in his blanket, and steal softly to the door of our lodge. Whisper my name, Nin-i-mo-sha, and I shall come out and tell you what to do."

"Nin-i-mo-sha," murmured the youth. "What a beautiful name!" Then, before he could thank her, the girls were gone.

Mish-o-sha now appeared, and made a sign to Seegwun to join him. The old man seemed to be in a good humor, and passed the time telling stories; but Seegwun was not deceived by this pretense of friendship. When the Magician was sound asleep, he rose, wrapped Mish-o-sha's blanket around him, and walked carefully to the door of the little lodge.

"Nin-i-mo-sha!" he whispered, and his heart beat fast; for Nin-i-mo-sha in the Indian tongue is "My Sweetheart."

"Seegwun!" she answered; and his name, meaning "Spring," came like music from her lips.

She drew aside the curtain, and came out.

"Here," she said, "is food that will last your brother for several days. Get into Mish-o-sha's canoe, pronounce the magic charm, and it will take you where you wish. You can be back before daybreak."

"But the owl?" asked Seegwun. "Will he not cry out?"

"Walk with a stoop, the way Mish-o-sha walks," she explained. "Ko-ko-ko-ho, when he sees you, will cry 'Hoot, hoot!' You must answer, 'Hoot, hoot, whoo! Mish-o-sha.' Then he will let you pass."

Seegwun did as he was told, and was soon skimming across the lake. Having landed on the beach, he began to bark like a squirrel; and at this friendly signal his brother ran up and flung his arms around him. Seegwun made a shelter for the boy, and told him he would come again. Then he returned in the canoe, and was soon fast asleep in the Magician's lodge.

Mish-o-sha, who trusted in his owl, suspected nothing. How should he know what lovers can do when they put their heads together?

"You have slept well, my son," said he. "And now we

"Hoot, hoot, whoo! Mish-o-sha!"

have a pleasant journey before us. We are going to an island where thousands of gulls lay their eggs in the sand, and we shall get all we can carry away."

Remembering what Nin-i-mo-sha had said, Seegwun shivered. But she kissed her hand, and waved him a good-bye; and this put heart in him.

As the canoe sped away, he made sure that his hunting knife slipped easily in its sheath, and he did not take his eyes off Mish-o-sha for a moment.

When they reached the island the gulls rose in great numbers, and flew screaming above their heads.

"You gather the eggs," said the Magician, "while I keep watch in the canoe."

Seegwun hastened ashore, glad to quit the old man's company. Then the Magician cried out to the gulls:

He seized the first bird that attacked him.

"Ho, my feathered friends! Here is the human offering I promised you when you agreed to call me master. Fly down, my pretty ones! Fly down, and devour him!"

Striking the side of his canoe, he abandoned the youth to the mercy of the birds.

With harsh cries, the gulls swept down on Seegwun. Never had he heard such a clamor. Ten thousand wings beat the air, and stirred it like a storm. Whirling and darting they came upon him in a cloud. But Seegwun did not flinch. Shouting the *Saw-saw-quan*, or war-cry, he seized the first bird that attacked him. Then grasping it by the neck, he held it high above his head in his left hand, and with his right hand drew his knife, which glittered in the sun.

"Hold!" he cried. "Hold, you poor fools! Beware the vengeance of the Great Spirit."

The gulls paused in their attack, but still circled around him, with sharp beaks extended.

"Hear me, O Gulls!" he continued. "The Great Spirit gave you life that you might serve mankind. Slay me, and you slay one made to rule over all the beasts and birds. I tell you, beware!"

"But Mish-o-sha is all powerful," screamed the gulls. "He has bidden us destroy you."

"Mish-o-sha is no Manito," answered Seegwun. "He is only a wicked magician who would use you for his own evil ends. Bear me on your wings back to his island; for it is he who must be destroyed."

Then the gulls, persuaded that Mish-o-sha had tricked them, drew close together, that the youth might lie upon their backs. Rising on the wind, they carried him across the waters, setting him down gently by the lodge before the Magician had arrived there.

Nin-i-mo-sha rejoiced when she saw it was really Seegwun. "I was not mistaken in you," she told him. "It is plain that the Great Spirit protects you. But Mish-o-sha will try again, so be on your guard."

The Magician now arrived in his magic canoe. When he saw Seegwun he tried to smile pleasantly. But having had little practice in thinking kind thoughts, he only grinned like a gargoyle, which, excepting perhaps the hyena, has the most painful possible smile.

"Good, my son!" he managed to say. "You must not misunderstand me. I did it to test your courage; and now Nin-i-mo-sha is sure to love you. Ah, my children, you will make a happy pair!"

Nin-i-mo-sha turned away to hide her disgust, but Seegwun pretended to believe the malicious old man was in earnest.

"However," continued the Magician, "I owe you something for having seemed to play you such a trick. I see you wear no ornaments. Come with me, then, to the Island of Glittering Shells, and soon you will be attired as becomes a handsome warrior."

The island where they landed was indeed a wonderful place, covered with colored shells that gleamed in the sun like jewels.

"Look!" said Mish-o-sha, as they walked along the beach. "Out there a little way. See it shining on the bottom."

Seegwun waded in. When the water reached his thighs, the Magician made a leap for the canoe, and shoved it far out into the lake.

"Come, King of Fishes!" he called. "You have always served me well. Here is your reward."

Then, striking his canoe, he quickly disappeared.

Immediately an enormous fish, with jaws wide open, rose to the surface a few feet away. But Seegwun only smiled, saying as he drew his long blade:

"Know, Monster, that I am Seegwun—named after him whose breath warms the ice-bound waters and clothes the hills with green. The cowardly Mish-o-sha, fearing the anger of the Great Spirit, seeks to make you do what he dares not do himself. Spill but one drop of my blood, and it will dye the waters of the lake, in which all your tribe will miserably perish."

"Mish-o-sha has deceived me," said the King of Fishes. "He promised me a tender maiden, and has brought instead a youth with the eyes of a warrior. How shall I aid you, my Master?"

"Wretch!" exclaimed Seegwun. "Rejoice that he did

not keep his frightful promise. You deserve to die at my hands, but I give you a chance to repent. Take me on your back to the island of Mish-o-sha, and I will spare your life."

The King of Fishes hastened to take Seegwun astride his broad back, and swam so swiftly that he reached

The King of Fishes hastened to take him astride his back.

the island soon after Mish-o-sha. The Magician was explaining to Nin-i-mo-sha how the youth had fallen from the canoe into the jaws of a big fish, when along came Seegwun himself, strolling up from the Lake as if he had returned from an everyday excursion. Even so, Mish-o-sha still sought to excuse himself.

"My daughter," said he. "I was only trying to find out how much you cared for him."

But all the while he was saying to himself that the next time he would not fail. And the next time was the very next day.

"My owl is growing old, and cannot live much longer," he explained. "I should like to catch a young eagle, and tame him. Will you help me?"

Seegwun consented, and went with him in the magic canoe to a rocky point of land reaching out into the lake. There, in the fork of a tall pine, was an eagle's nest, in which were some young eagles, who could not yet fly.

"Quick!" said Mish-o-sha. "Climb the tree before the old birds return."

Seegwun had almost reached the nest when the Magician spoke to the pine, commanding it to grow taller. At once it began to rise, until it was so high, and swayed so in the wind, that he felt it would take all his courage to get down again. At the same time the Magician uttered a peculiar cry, at which the father and mother eagles came swooping from the clouds to protect their young.

"Ho, ho!" laughed Mish-o-sha. "This time I have made no mistake. Either you will fall and break your neck, or the eagles will scratch your eyes out."

Striking his canoe, he vanished in the mist.

The eagles now circled around Seegwun, who, resting on a branch, thus addressed them:

"My brothers, behold the eagle's feather in my hair! It proves my admiration for your bravery and skill. Yet in me you see your master; for I am a man, and you are only birds. Obey me, then, and bear me to Mish-o-sha's island."

This praise pleased the eagles, who respected the youth's cool courage. Mounting on the back of the enormous male bird, Seegwun was borne through the air, and set down safely on the enchanted island.

Mish-o-sha now saw that neither bird nor beast would harm this handsome youth, who seemed to be

Seegwun was borne through the air.

protected by some powerful Manito. It must be done some other way.

"One more test," he said to Seegwun, "and then you may take Nin-i-mo-sha for your wife. But first you must prove your skill as a hunter. Come!"

They made a lodge in the forest; and Mish-o-sha, by his magic, caused a snow-storm, with a stinging gale from the north, like a flight of icy arrows. Seegwun, that night, before going to sleep, had hung his moccasins and leggings by the fire to dry; and Mish-o-sha, rising first, at daybreak, took one of each and threw them into the flames. Then he rubbed his hands, and laughed like a prairie wolf.

"What is it?" asked Seegwun, sitting up.

"Alas, my son!" said Mish-o-sha. "I was just too late. This is the season of the moon when fire attracts all things. It has drawn to it one of your moccasins and leggings, and destroyed them. *Yeo, yeo!* I should have warned you."

Seegwun held his tongue, though the thing was plain enough. Mish-o-sha meant that he should freeze to death. But Seegwun, praying silently to his Manito for aid, took from the fireplace a charred stick with which he blackened one leg and foot, murmuring at the same time a charm. Then putting on his remaining moccasin and legging, he was ready for the hunt.

Their way led through snow and ice, into thickets of thorn, and over bogs half-frozen, where Seegwun sank to the knees. But his prayer had been heard; the charm worked, and the youth walked on, dry shod. With his first arrow he slew a bear.

"Now," he said, looking the Magician full in the eye. "I see you are suffering from the cold. Let us go back to your island."

At Seegwun's bold look, Mish-o-sha bent his head, and mumbled some foolish answer. At last he had met his match; and he knew it.

"Take up the bear on your shoulders!" commanded Seegwun.

Again the Magician obeyed. For the first time they returned together to the island, where the two young girls looked on in amazement to see the proud Mish-o-sha staggering under the weight of the bear, grunting with helpless rage.

"His power is broken," agreed Nin-i-mo-sha, when Seegwun had told her all. "But we shall never sleep in safety until we are really rid of him. What is best to do?"

They put their heads together; and when they had talked it over, Nin-i-mo-sha laughed merrily.

"He deserves a greater punishment," she said. "The world will not be safe as long as he has life. Yet what we plan to do will revenge us, without shedding a single drop of blood."

The next day Seegwun said to the Magician:

"It is time that we rescued my brother, whom we left all alone on the beach. Come with me."

Mish-o-sha made a wry face, but prepared to go. Landing on the beach, they soon spied the boy, who joyfully clambered into the canoe. Then Seegwun said to the old man:

"Those red willows over on the bank would make good smoking mixture. Could you manage to climb up there and cut me some?"

"To be sure, my son, to be sure," answered Mish-o-sha, walking rapidly toward the willows. "I am not so weak and good-for-nothing as you seem to think."

Seegwun struck the canoe with his hand, pronouncing the magic words, *Chemaun Poll*; and away it went with the two brothers aboard, leaving the Magician high and dry, and gnashing his yellow teeth.

The girls ran to meet them at the shore, Nin-i-mo-sha rejoicing that the old man had been left behind, while her sister could think of nothing but the attractive boy who looked so much like his big brother.

"But Mish-o-sha can call the canoe back to him," said Nin-i-mo-sha, "until a way is found to break the charm. Someone must keep watch, with his hand upon it."

Ioscoda begged permission to do his part; so they left him, with night coming on, sitting on the sand and holding fast to the canoe.

It was a tiresome task for a little boy already weary with long waiting. To amuse himself he began to count the stars. First he counted those in the Big Dipper and the Little Dipper, then the ones that look like a high-back chair, and the three big bright ones in the belt of Orion the Hunter. He did not know them by these

They left him holding fast to the canoe.

names, which were given them long afterward; but he recognized the cluster called O-jeeg An-nung, the Fisher, who brought Summer from the sky because his boy was cold.

Ioscoda also was cold, sitting there in the wet sand. But Indian boys do not complain. Yet seeing the Fisher stars, he thought of his own dear father, and wondered where he might be. Had Ioscoda been a white boy, instead of a red, we think the sand he sat on might have been a little wetter for his tears. As it was, he found himself looking at the sky through a kind of fog. What was it? He rubbed his eyes, lost his count, and began all over again.

The worst of it was that Indians could reckon only with their fingers—unless you include their toes; and Ioscoda's toes were tucked away snugly in his moccasins, quite out of sight and question. How many fingers had he counted—and how—many—stars—?

The fog, or whatever it was, filled his eyes. Lap, lap! went the little waves, rocking the canoe like a cradle. Soo, soo! sighed the wind in the cedars. All else earthly nodded and was still; even the stars blinked and winked, as if weary of watching the world.

And Ioscoda slept.

Whoo, whoo! The cry of Ko-ko-ko-ho, the owl, shrilled evilly on the ears. It was only for a moment. The shadows lifted, a squirrel barked. Wa-bun, the East Wind, rising above the rim of the waters, let loose his silver arrows. It was day.

Ioscoda sat up, only half aroused, and looked out over the lake. Was he still on the wild beach, waiting for his brother? Then he remembered, and gave a guilty start. The canoe was gone!

Gone, but come again! There it appeared, gliding straight toward him; and in it sat Mish-o-sha.

"Good-morning, child!" called the Magician, as the canoe grated on the sand. "Are you not glad to see your grandfather again?"

Ioscoda clenched his small fists. He was very brave, and he was angry.

"You are *not* my grandfather," he said, "and I am *not* glad to see you again."

"*Esa, esa!* (Shame, shame!)" chuckled the old man. "But Seegwun will be glad to see me, and so will my dear daughters. I hope they have not been worried about me."

He was much pleased with his cleverness in outwitting them all, and was now as impudent as before. But Seegwun bided his time. He thought of another plan.

"Grandfather," said he, "it seems that we must continue to live here together. Let us therefore lay in a sup-

ply of meat for the winter. Come with me to the mainland. I am sure you must be a mighty hunter."

Mish-o-sha's vanity was his weakest point.

"*Eh, yah!*" he answered, boastfully. "I can run all day
with a dead deer on my back. I have done it."

"Good!" said Seegwun. "The wind is going north
again, and we shall need all our strength on the march."

Now Seegwun had somehow learned the Magician's
dearest secret, which was this: Mish-o-sha's left leg and
foot were the only parts of his body that could be
harmed. No arrow could pierce his heart; a war-club
brought down upon his head would be shivered into
splinters. As well strike him with a straw. But his left leg
and foot. Ah! It was not for rheumatism that his legging
was so well laced. And *why* did he always sit down with
his left foot tucked up under him? Ha! Why, indeed?
Seegwun had found the answer.

They made a rude lodge in the forest, just as they had
done before. And again it came bitter cold; only this
time it was Seegwun that brought the storm. He could
not help laughing. There was the blazing fire, and there
on the couch was Mish-o-sha, sound asleep.

Seegwun softly rose, took both the Magician's moccasins and leggings, and threw them into the flames.

"Get up, grandfather," he called. "It's the season
when fire attracts all things, and I fear you have lost
something you may need."

When Mish-o-sha saw what had happened he looked
so frightened that Seegwun was almost sorry for him.
But remembering Nin-i-mo-sha and his little brother, he
could think of no other way. "We must be going," he
said.

They set out through the snow. My, how cold it was!
Mish-o-sha began to run, thinking this would help;
while Seegwun followed, fearing that if he led, the Ma-

They set out through the snow.

gician might send an arrow through his back. After running for an hour, the Magician was quite out of breath, and his legs and feet were growing numb and stiff.

They had come to the edge of the forest, and reached the shore of the lake. Here Mish-o-sha stopped. When he tried to take another step, he could not lift his feet. How heavy they had grown! He tried again; but something strange had happened. His toes sank into the sand, and took the form of roots. The feathers in his hair, and then the hair itself, changed gradually into leaves. His outstretched arms were branches, swaying in the wind; bark appeared on his body.

Seegwun looked and wondered. That which had been Mish-o-sha was no longer a man, but a tree, a sycamore hung with button-balls, leaning crookedly toward the lake.

At last the wicked old Magician had met his master.

Mish-o-sha was no longer a man.

No more would his evil spell be cast on the young and innocent. Seegwun lingered a moment, to make sure that Mish-o-sha would not come to life. Then he took his way across the water, where the others, anxiously awaiting him, were told the good news.

"Mish-o-sha is no more," said Seegwun. "He can never harm us again. Let us leave this place where we have suffered so much, and make our home on the mainland."

So together they went forth, his sweetheart, her sister, and the boy, with Seegwun showing the way. The trail he took led them again to the great forest, and once more to the lodge from which he had set out. And there they lived happily for the rest of their days.